jumping
the
scratch

SARAH WEEKS

jumping
the
scratch

LAURA GERINGER BOOKS
An Imprint of HarperCollins*Publishers*

Jumping the Scratch
Copyright © 2006 by Sarah Weeks

Library of Congress Cataloging-in-Publication Data
Weeks, Sarah
    Jumping the scratch / Sarah Weeks.— 1st ed.
      p. cm.
    Summary: After moving with his mother to a
trailer park to care for an injured aunt, eleven-year-
old Jamie Reardon struggles to cope with a deeply
buried secret.
     ISBN-10: 0-06-054109-1 (trade bdg.)
     ISBN-13: 978-0-06-054109-5 (trade bdg.)
     ISBN-10: 0-06-054110-5 (lib. bdg.)
     ISBN-13: 978-0-06-054110-1 (lib. bdg.)
    [1. Memory—Fiction. 2. Aunts—Fiction. 3. Child
sexual abuse—Fiction.] I. Title.
PZ7.W42215Jum 2006
[Fic]—dc22   2005017776
                            CIP
                            AC

Typography by
Karin Paprocki

1   2   3   4   5   6   7   8   9   10
❖
First Edition

To my amazing Austin friends, Amy, David, Hannah, and Beth Roberts

With special thanks to Laura Geringer, Jill Santopolo, Nancy Princenthal, Joseph LeDoux, Tom Wilinsky, Dan Lebson, and as always, David

jumping
the
scratch

1 ∴

I HAVE A PRETTY GOOD MEMORY, BUT IT'S GOT A MIND of its own. It has never been very interested in holding on to anything having to do with numbers or spelling or ways of knowing when it's appropriate to use a semicolon. It's impossible to predict what it will decide is important. Sometimes whole years of my life have whizzed by and very little of what's happened has stuck. But there is one year I remember in such vivid detail, I sometimes feel as though I'm still in the middle of it even though it all happened a long time ago.

I was eleven years old and in the fifth grade at Pine Tree Elementary when Arthur came to visit. I didn't see what the big fuss was about. Just because some guy named Arthur was coming to our class, we were supposed to wear our best clothes and be on our best behavior and not shout out and a lot of other things I didn't bother to listen to when Miss Miller told us about his coming. I didn't listen to much of anything she said that year. I wasn't interested, and I didn't care. Looking back on it now, I guess that might have had something to do with why she was always yelling at me.

"Are you listening, James? *Best* behavior," Miss Miller said, giving me the big fisheye.

My name is not James; it's Jamie. It says so right on my birth certificate, but I never bothered to tell Miss Miller that. Somehow it seemed right for her to call me by the wrong name. She didn't have any idea who I was.

That day, while she talked on and on about Arthur's visit, I did what I always did: reached back with my thumbs and plugged my earholes closed. But Miss Miller's voice found its way inside my head somehow anyway, like smoke curling under a locked door. Arthur this. Arthur that. I pressed my thumbs down harder, then let go. Open, closed, open, closed, faster and faster until it chopped up the words like cabbage for slaw and made it sound like she was speaking Chinese. I just kept doing that until she was done talking and it was finally time for us to go home.

I hated everything about that year in Miss Miller's class. We'd moved to Traverse City in November, two months after the school year had begun, and by the time spring rolled around, I still hadn't made a single friend. It was my own fault. It's hard for people to like you when you can't stand yourself.

"Best clothes," Miss Miller had said. That was a joke. I had two kinds of clothes at home: clean and dirty. I didn't plan on telling my mother what Miss Miller had said. I knew she would just say, "Make do, Jamie." She said that all the time after we moved in with my aunt Sapphy, at the Wondrous Acres trailer park on the south side of town.

Wondrous Acres was anything but wondrous. Ours was the fifth trailer in a line of fifteen single-wides that sat on a flat strip of asphalt baking in the sun or rattling in the wind depending on the season. Some of the trailers had names over their doors instead of numbers, Tin Heaven and Dolly's Spot. Ours was just plain old number five, but if it had been mine to name, I would have called it Make Do.

We had a real house back when we lived in Battle Creek. I had a room of my own and, best of all, a cat named Mister. Mister was just a stray, somebody else's cat that had run away, but after I fed him tuna fish and milk, he didn't run away from me, so my mom said she guessed he was mine. Mister was the first friend I had who liked me best. He didn't like anybody else to pick him up or even touch him. He slept on my pillow at night. I'd lie in the dark, rubbing him behind his soft black ears, telling him everything, while he lay there purring until I was all talked out. I can close my eyes and, to this day, still recall the way Mister smelled behind his ears.

One night Mister didn't come home. I called and called for him, but he didn't come.

"Probably out looking for some female companionship," my dad told me. "Can't blame a fella for wanting a little of that now, can you?" Then he winked at me and laughed until his breath ran out and he had to cough. My mother shot him one of her looks, but she didn't say anything.

With some people you can tell when they're mad, because they yell at you and say things they try to take back later on, but my mother is the opposite. The madder she gets, the less she says. I don't remember her saying much of anything that whole last year in Battle Creek.

The next morning when Mister still hadn't come back, I went out to try to find him. It didn't take long. He was lying on his side out in the ditch beside the road in front of my house. At first I thought he was sleeping, but when I picked him up, I knew right away that he was dead. I sat there by the road for a while, holding him and telling him how sorry I was that I hadn't been there to protect him. Then I took him inside, wrapped him up in a blue and white checkered dish towel, and put him in a shoe box along with a couple of cans of tuna. I got a shovel out of the garage, dug a hole, and buried him out in the backyard. Then I cried so hard, my eyes swelled shut and it looked like somebody had punched me in the face.

My dad must have heard me crying, because he came out to see what was the matter. I told him about Mister, and he said something about how he was just an old stray anyway, and there were plenty more where that one had come from. I guess he was trying to make me feel better, but instead I got mad and told him to go away, just go away.

It was about a week later that my dad took off with a cashier from the MicroMart, leaving my mother and me to fend for ourselves. There's a saying about bad things coming in threes. When the call came a couple of months later that my aunt Sapphy had been seriously injured in a freak accident at the cherry factory where she worked, my mom told me we were moving to Traverse City to live with her until she got better. I figured that was the third and final bad thing in the series. As it turned out, though, either the saying was off by one, or that particular misfortune wasn't meant to count as one of my three, because there was one more bad thing still in store for me.

We had a big yard sale and sold off most of the furniture and kitchen stuff, and a week before Thanksgiving my mom and I packed what was left into a U-Haul and left the house in Battle Creek for good. I thought about digging Mister up so I could bring him along and rebury him in my new backyard. It didn't seem right to leave him behind. But then I remembered how he had felt in my hands when I'd lifted him out of the ditch. How light he had been. Like the most important part of him wasn't there anymore. And I realized there was no point in digging up that shoe box, because I was the one who was about to be left behind.

∶ 2

"HEY, REAR-END!" LARRY BAYWOOD CALLED OUT when I got to the bus stop after school that day. "How's your crack?"

There were hoots of laughter from the crowd of kids standing around on the curb. They'd heard this routine before, and they loved it.

The yellow school bus pulled up, the folding doors banged open, and I got on, taking my usual seat in the back. I pulled a dog-eared copy of *The Hobbit* out of my backpack and opened it to a random page in the middle. I'm not a big fantasy buff—I prefer books about real people and real life—but it didn't matter because I wasn't reading *The Hobbit*. I never read for real on the bus, I only pretended to; it wasn't safe to read.

I'm sure there were plenty of perfectly nice kids on that bus (I know for a fact there was at least one), but it's Larry Baywood's shadow that falls across most of my memories of those long bus rides to and from school that year. Larry was ugly inside and out, with one of those pushed-in kinds of faces that look like a crushed pop can. His front teeth were chipped, and he had a lazy eye that sometimes rolled off to the side like a pool ball gliding toward a side pocket. Even so, nobody ever called him by anything other than his given name.

When he found out my last name was Reardon and he started calling me Rear-end, I came up with an insulting nickname for him too. Padiddle—on account of his lazy eye. Padiddle was what my dad used to say when we passed a car with only one headlight working. But kids like me weren't allowed to call kids like Larry Baywood names. Nobody had to tell me that; it was one of those things you just know.

In Battle Creek I never got picked on. I didn't stick out. I could throw and catch a ball; I wasn't too big or too small; I didn't talk funny or have a donkey laugh. We had an expression back home, because of the Kellogg factory's being there in town, "normal as cornflakes," and that was me. But when we moved to Traverse City, suddenly I was different.

At first it was just because I was new, but it wasn't long before there was something else that set me apart.

I didn't tell a soul when it happened, not even my mother. I pushed it down, deep inside, and tried as hard as I could to forget it. I kept my mouth shut, and I was careful not to look people in the eye. What I really wanted was to be invisible, and there were plenty of people who were perfectly happy to treat me as if I were. Unfortunately, Larry Baywood wasn't one of them.

My father used to take me fishing for bluegills at a pond near our house. One time I remember it was hot and the fish weren't biting, so he told me I could swim in my underwear instead if I wanted to. I was laughing and splashing up a storm when my father pointed and told me to look up. Five big turkey buzzards were slowly circling overhead.

"Where'd they come from?" I asked.

"Heard you splashing and figured on some easy pickings," he told me.

Old or lame animals, he explained, sometimes come to the water to drink or roll in the mud. Their splashing attracts the buzzards, which come and circle, hoping the animal will die and provide an easy meal. I didn't feel much like swimming after that.

Larry Baywood reminded me of those turkey buzzards. He sensed easy pickings and was always circling overhead.

"I asked you a question, Rear-end," Larry said once the bus had started moving. "How's your crack?"

I didn't look at him. Just pretended to read my book. Out of the corner of my eye I noticed the edge of a foil gum wrapper sticking out from between the cushions of the seat next to me, and slowly I slid my hand over and covered it with my thumb.

"What's the matter with you?" Larry asked. "Did you eat glue or something?"

He got out of his seat and started lurching down the aisle toward me, using the seat backs to help him keep his balance. I felt the back of my neck prickle, but I sat there silently, holding my book and trying not to choke on the sickeningly sweet butterscotch taste that had begun to fill my mouth.

"You can get a dog to open his mouth up by squeezing his cheeks together, did you know that, Rear-end? Do you want me to come squeeze your cheeks so you can open up and answer my question?" Larry asked.

About the last thing I wanted was for Larry Baywood to come squeeze my cheeks, but still I just sat there pretending to read. Everybody was howling and egging him on as Larry looked around, grinning proudly, happy to take credit for providing the entertainment for that afternoon's ride. I swallowed butterscotch and waited for it to be over.

Butterscotch always came first. And after that the sensation of the button pressing its smooth round reminder into my cheek. I didn't get past butterscotch that day, though. Some commotion in the front of the bus distracted Larry Baywood from his purpose, and he clomped back up the aisle to be with his friends. As soon as he was gone, I lifted my thumb and carefully pulled the gum wrapper out from between the seat cushions. After smoothing it on my knee first, I stuck it between the pages of my book for safekeeping. Then I rode the rest of the way home pretending to read and wondering if I would ever feel normal again.

A few other people got off at the same stop as I did every day, including Audrey Krouch. She was in my class, and like me, she lived in Wondrous Acres. I didn't know her, and I didn't want to. I didn't like girls, and besides, she was strange. She smelled funny, like fried onions, and her bangs were cut too short, making her pasty-white forehead look huge. The strangest thing about her, though, was the glasses she wore. They were men's black plastic frames, way too wide for her face, and they didn't have any lenses in them. You could have stuck your fingers right through the holes and poked her in the eyes if you'd wanted to. Miss Miller wouldn't let her wear the glasses during school hours, but in the morning, waiting for the bus to come, she always had them on, and after school she wore them too.

I always made it a point to be the last one to get off the bus when it stopped. I had learned the hard way that it was safer to be behind someone going down the steps than the other way around. Audrey got off ahead of me and headed up the driveway, but I took my usual route, walking along the ditch beside the road for a while before cutting through the weeds and angling up the hill toward home. Just as I stepped off the road, I heard a rustling sound. I jumped back and had to clap my hand over my mouth to muffle a cry as a long black snake with yellow stripes shot out from under my foot and disappeared into the tall grass.

"Garter," I whispered, my heart still thumping hard from the shock. I hate snakes, and that field was full of them, but I didn't have a choice. It was the only way home.

3 :•

"WHO'S THAT?" MY AUNT SAPPHY CALLED FROM THE back of the trailer a few minutes later as I came in, letting the screen door bang closed behind me.

My grandmother had three daughters, all of whom she named after gems. Emerald is the oldest; my mother, Opal, is the baby; and in between is Sapphire, who everybody calls Sapphy.

Sapphy is the only sister who never got married. She started working at the cherry factory right out of high school. Aunt Emmy married a truck driver named Perry Chizek, who took her away to live with him in Florida. My mom married my dad, moved to Battle Creek, and then had me. But Sapphy stayed in Traverse City, living at home with her parents in the same room she'd shared with her sisters growing up. She helped take care of my grandpa Will until he died, and she nursed my grandma Jeanne when she got sick too.

It's only about a four-hour drive from Traverse City to Battle Creek, so we went up there fairly often to visit, and Sapphy and my grandparents would drive down to see us too. I loved when they came to our house, because Sapphy would sleep in my room. I gladly gave up my bed and slept beside her on the floor in a sleeping bag. We'd lie there in the dark, talking quietly long after everyone else in the house had gone to sleep. Sometimes Sapphy would tell me funny things she and my mother had done when they were little, like dressing their dog up in a nightgown, wheeling him around in a baby carriage, and telling the neighbors Grandma Jeanne had just had another baby. Sometimes I told her about the arguments I overheard my parents having or the strange dream I had over and over again that something was chasing me and then just as I was about to be caught, a giant bird would swoop down out of nowhere and rescue me, lifting me high up into the sky and carrying me off to safety. Sapphy would prop herself up with her pillows, and even though it was dark, I could see her bright eyes shining and her head tilted slightly to the side like a crow as she listened. If I could have kept my eyes open, I would have wanted to stay awake all night talking with Sapphy. She was like Mister: She knew how to listen, and I felt I could tell her anything.

When my grandma Jeanne died, Aunt Sapphy found out she and Grandpa Will hadn't paid their taxes in years. Between what the government said they owed and what the First National Bank of Traverse City laid claim to, the only thing of value left, once the dust settled, was twelve place settings of my grandmother's good bone china. Each sister got four place settings, and Sapphy got to keep the gravy boat. I guess that was her reward for having stayed there until the bitter end. The real estate agent who handled selling the house told Sapphy it was going to be hard to find a buyer because of the smell.

"Death leaves a lingering odor," she said.

"So does life," Sapphy told her.

Sapphy packed up and moved to the trailer in Wondrous Acres, where she lived by herself for a few years until she had her accident at the cherry factory. One minute she was standing there watching cherries go by on the conveyor belt, and the next thing she knew, she was lying in a hospital bed with her head all bandaged up. She doesn't remember a thing about how it happened. She woke up in the hospital with a terrible headache, her hair shaved clean off, and twenty-seven stitches marching like a line of black ants across her scalp. We were told that a big metal pipe had come loose and fallen from the ceiling, hitting Sapphy square on the top of her head.

While she was still in the hospital, a lawyer came to visit, and Sapphy signed a bunch of papers. After that, instead of a paycheck she got a disability check from the Cheery Cherry Corporation every month. The check wasn't huge, but it was big enough to mean she didn't have to work anymore. Even so, she couldn't have kept living in the trailer. At least not by herself. After the accident Sapphy was missing more than just her hair.

It was as if somebody had come into her head with a little pink eraser and gone to town rubbing things out. Not remembering the accident wouldn't have been so bad if that had been all there was to it. But the blow to her head caused Sapphy's memory to develop a skip, like an old phonograph record with a scratch. Although she could remember very clearly everything from her past right up until the moment the pipe fell, she lost the ability to make any new memories. Things that happened after the accident stayed with her only for about half an hour, and then they faded away just as if they'd never happened.

I once saw an episode of *The Three Stooges* where Moe got hit in the head by a falling flowerpot and lost his memory. He couldn't remember his own name or recognize the other stooges at all. He staggered around in a daze, seeing stars and hearing birds tweeting, until Curly accidentally hit him in the head with a long board and suddenly Moe was cured.

In real life amnesia doesn't work like that. Sapphy didn't forget her name, and she knew who my mom and I were when we came and saw her in the hospital. But if I told her a good joke, she'd laugh her head off, and half an hour later not only would she have forgotten the punch line, but she wouldn't remember that I'd ever told her the joke.

I knew better than to believe hitting Sapphy in the head a second time would cure her, but I sure wished it could be that easy. I felt sorry for her, but I remember thinking she was lucky at least in one respect: She wasn't to blame for her misfortune.

That pipe would have fallen no matter what. She couldn't help it if she was standing under it when it happened. It wasn't her fault. But I was the one who let Mister outside that night, and I was the one who told my father to go away, and when Old Gray asked me what my favorite candy was, I was the one who told him butterscotch.

4 ⦂

IN SPITE OF WHAT HAD HAPPENED TO SAPPHY, RIGHT after we got to Traverse City my mother took a job herself at the Cheery Cherry canning factory. She didn't have any choice; it was the only place in town that was hiring. She worked the late shift because it paid more, but it meant I barely saw her. She went to work at eight o'clock at night and didn't come home until four the next morning. It was pitch-dark when she came in, and she was always careful not to wake me as she tiptoed through the kitchen and on into the back where her room was. When I got up in the morning, I'd find my toothbrush laid out on the edge of the bathroom sink with a fresh stripe of toothpaste she'd squeezed onto it for me.

Money was tight. The only extras my mother allowed herself were cartons of menthol Kools and six-packs of diet cola because she was addicted to both. Every day she sent me to school with a bag lunch containing a peanut butter sandwich, a can opener, and a can of cherries with a damaged label, which she got for free at work. The cherries were for dessert, and I was supposed to use the juice to help wash down the sandwich.

"Two birds with one stone," she told me.

Eating cherries day after day, I developed a deep hatred for them, but at least later on I found a use for the empty cans.

In case you don't know, northern Michigan is cherry country. Seventy-five percent of the country's tart cherries are grown there. Whether they want to or not, anybody who ever lives in northern Michigan carries around a bushel of cherry facts in his head for life. Here's another one: The average cherry tree produces approximately seven thousand cherries a year, which is enough to make twenty-eight deep-dish cherry pies.

There was no TV reception at Wondrous Acres, so it wasn't even worth trying to watch. We had a radio, though. When I got up, I'd turn that on low so I wouldn't wake anybody, tune in one of the Detroit stations, and read while I ate my breakfast alone at the little table in the corner of the kitchen.

That year I became what I guess you would call a reader. I took tons of books out of the library at school, plus I read whatever my mother left lying around, even the sappy paperback romance novels she bought off the spinning wire racks at Kresge's. I read because the words made noise, and the noise filled my head, and that gave me at least a little break from having to think about the dumb things I'd done to mess up what had been a perfectly good, normal-as-cornflakes life.

That afternoon, I was standing at the counter, pouring myself a glass of milk, when Sapphy appeared, wearing her pajamas and a nubby old pink robe. Her hair had grown back, but it was uneven and short, and she didn't like to comb it because she said it hurt her head. She always looked like she'd just woken up, and the only time she ever bothered to get dressed was when my mother took her downtown to see the doctor.

"Is that you, Jamie?" Sapphy said. "Golly, how you've grown. What on earth are you doing here, sweet thing? I wasn't expecting you, was I?"

I was used to this. Sapphy was always surprised to see me when I came home from school each day,

23

even though my mom and I had been living there with her for months. I opened *The Hobbit*, pulled out the gum wrapper I'd found on the bus, and handed it to her.

"I brought you something," I said.

She laughed.

"I used to collect these when I was a little girl, did you know that?" she said, taking the wrapper from me and holding it up to admire it as if it were something special.

"He knows about your wrappers," said Marge, coming into the room with a gossip magazine in one hand and one of my mother's diet colas in the other. "We *all* know about your wrappers."

Marge was the home nursing aide. She came every morning before I left for school to watch over Sapphy while my mother was sleeping, and she stayed until five, except on the weekends. Marge never came right out and said it, but I don't think she liked any of us very much, especially not Sapphy. The insurance company paid for her to come, and we needed the help, but I hated the way she treated Sapphy. I wished the insurance company would pay for me to stay home from school and take care of her instead.

"I'm sorry. Do I know you?" Sapphy asked, looking at Marge as though she'd never in her life laid eyes on her before.

"Here we go again." Marge sighed. "You know me, and I know you too. Now let's go have a pill, and while we wait for it to kick in, you can add that wrapper to your chain."

Sapphy looked confused, but she let Marge take her by the arm and lead her back to her room.

"You can't be talking about that old gum wrapper chain I used to have. I haven't seen that thing in years," Sapphy said.

"Uh-huh. Not since this morning," said Marge.

Both Sapphy and my mother had collected gum wrappers back when they were kids. They'd used only the silver foil part of the wrappers, folding and hooking them together into zigzaggy chains. There had been a fierce competition between the two of them to see whose chain would get to be the longest. My mother's got lost or thrown out at some point along the way, but not long after we moved into the trailer, we found Sapphy's gum wrapper chain curled up in the corner of an old box of junk high up on a shelf in the back of one of the closets.

Sapphy's accident had made her unsteady on her feet and clumsy with her hands. It was my mother's idea for her to work on the wrapper chain to help improve her coordination. Sapphy seemed to enjoy it. It brought back pleasant memories for her, and she would reminisce, telling the same stories over and over again without realizing we'd heard them all before.

The wrapper chain was kept on a hook on the back of Sapphy's door. She liked the way the light from the little window over her bed caught in the folded foil and made it sparkle on sunny days. She liked anything that sparkled. I read somewhere that crows are like that too. If you leave a diamond ring outside on your windowsill, a crow will fly right down and steal it if you're not careful. I think maybe Sapphy was a crow in another life. She looked like one, the way she tilted her head when she listened, and she sure was crazy about those sparkly foil wrappers.

I carried my glass of milk out into the living room, pulled my math workbook out of my backpack, and started going over the homework problems. Pretty soon Marge appeared with a basket of dirty laundry in her arms.

"I'm going to go put a load in the machine," she said. "I won't have time to get it in the dryer before I leave, though. Can you remember to do that later?"

I was in the middle of trying to solve a difficult math problem.

"*Jamie!*" she said sharply. "I asked you a question. Can you please remember to put the laundry in the dryer?"

Have you ever noticed that some people take it personally when you don't answer their questions right when they ask them? Marge was like that, and so was Miss Miller. Whenever she called on me in class, she'd stand there, tapping her foot, saying, "I'm waiting, James. We're all waiting." I didn't understand why she called on me. It's not like I ever raised my hand. I didn't want to answer her questions, or Marge's questions either. Or anybody else's, for that matter.

:: 5

"WELL?" SAID MARGE IMPATIENTLY.

"I'll remember," I said.

"Laundry isn't supposed to be a part of this job," she complained as she dug around in the jar of change my mother kept on the counter, looking for quarters. "But somebody's got to do it, and as usual I guess it's gonna be me. Watch her while I'm gone, Jamie. You hear?"

Mister used to like to follow me around the house, purring and rubbing against my legs, but Sapphy would follow me around and talk.

"I know this is going to sound crazy," she said as she wandered out into the living room, where I was hunched over my workbook, still working on that same math problem, "but I don't remember getting this haircut. The last time I looked, I had a full head of hair, and now look at me. I look like a caveman. I've had the same gal doing my hair for umpteen years, and she's never done anything that looked like this before."

"They shaved your head at the hospital, Sapph," I told her. "You got hit in the head at the factory, and they shaved off your hair."

Sapphy looked surprised. She was always surprised when we told her about the accident.

"I got hit in the head?" she said.

I nodded. She touched her scalp with her fingertips and winced.

"No wonder it hurts," she said. "I thought I must have banged it on the corner of the medicine cabinet yesterday or something."

This discussion, word for word, including the part about the corner of the medicine cabinet, had taken place countless times. When it started, you had two choices. Either you could sit there and answer the questions about what had happened and when and how, or you could try to distract her.

"You want to play a game?" I said, opting for the latter and hoping to keep her occupied until Marge returned from the laundry shed.

"What game?" she asked, brightening a little.

Sapphy liked to play games. She told me she and

her sisters had played jacks and hopscotch and boxball as girls, and later she'd played bridge and Scrabble with Grandma Jeanne and Grandpa Will in the evenings to fill the long hours between dinnertime and bedtime. The game Sapphy and I played was called Use It or Lose It. I'd discovered it in a book I brought home from the school library. It was the only thing there about memory, and I checked it out several times.

There wasn't anything in it about amnesia, but I hadn't taken it out because I wanted to learn more about Sapphy's condition. I had taken it out for myself, hoping there might be something in it about learning how to forget. There were pages and pages of tips on how to improve your memory, but there wasn't one thing in there for someone like me who wanted to forget. At first I was discouraged, until it occurred to me that since remembering is the opposite of forgetting, maybe it would work if I just did the opposite of everything the book recommended.

That's why I gave up peanut butter. The book said it was a memory booster. I didn't bother to tell my mother I wanted a different kind of sandwich— I knew what she would say. Instead, every day at lunch I scraped out the peanut butter and ate only the bread. Playing the opposite of Use It or Lose It was a little trickier.

Here's how the game is supposed to work: Two players take turns being the *gatherer* and the *rememberer*. The gatherer goes around the house, picking up ten small objects, and puts them all together on a big plate or tray. Then the rememberer gets one minute to stare at the things on the tray, trying to commit them all to memory. When the minute is up, the gatherer tosses a dish towel over the items to cover them up, and then the rememberer has one minute to try to recall all ten things on the tray and write them down. Sapphy liked to play, but she wasn't very good at it. If I was the gatherer, and the ten things I chose were, say, a rubber band, a toothpick, a straw, a dime, a plastic spoon, a toothbrush, a sugar cube, a raisin, a cork, and a piece of string, and she was going to remember anything, it would probably be the dime—because it was shiny. If I put two shiny things on the tray, sometimes she would remember both of them and sometimes neither one. There was no way of telling with Sapphy.

When it was my turn to be the rememberer, I

tried to do the opposite and be the forgetter instead. I would stare at the objects on the tray and try as hard as I could to keep them from getting into my memory. But playing the game only pointed out what I already knew: No matter how hard you try, you can't force forgetting. It either happens on its own or it doesn't happen at all.

Marge hated the Use It or Lose It game. She'd always blame us when she couldn't find something she was looking for.

"Where's my glove?" she'd say, digging around in her pockets. "How many times have I told you not to use my stuff for that game?"

I never fessed up about using her stuff. After the game, when Marge wasn't paying attention, I would stuff the glove or whatever else I'd taken from her between the cushions of the couch or put it outside on the front steps, so she would find it later and think she'd dropped it there on her way in. I guess it was my way of getting back at her a little for the way she treated Sapphy.

Sapphy and I played Use It or Lose It until Marge returned from the laundry shed. As she came in the door carrying the empty basket, a car horn beeped twice down on the road.

"Mail's in," she said.

"What day is it?" Sapphy asked.

"Monday," Marge told her.

"Coupons!" said Sapphy happily.

Sapphy had always been a big coupon clipper. Mondays in Traverse City the Kroger circulars came, with a ten-page insert of three-color coupons. She had a coupon organizer file with cardboard tabs with headings like "BREAD AND CRACKERS," "DAIRY," "HOUSEHOLD CLEANERS," and "PET FOOD." Sapphy clipped coupons for Wonder bread and peanut butter and milk and other things we actually bought, but after a while we noticed that she was also clipping coupons for dog food and dishwasher soap.

"What are you doing?" my mother asked her once when she noticed Sapphy clipping out a coupon for Vet's Choice canned dog food. "We don't have a dog anymore, you know."

"I know that," she said, giving my mother a funny look. "What do you think I am, daft or something? Happy's been dead for over twenty years, Opal. Why would I be clipping coupons for him now?"

"I don't know, Sapph, I just thought maybe you'd forgotten."

"There's nothing wrong with my memory. I'm planning to get a dog from the pound," Sapphy said, filing the coupon behind the pet food tab. "I'm on the call list for a beagle or a cocker spaniel— whichever comes in first."

Judging from the coupons, apparently Sapphy was planning to get a dishwasher too. It was strange that she could remember plans she'd made for the future and she could remember the past, but she couldn't keep track of the present anymore. Her life was like one of my sandwiches, with the peanut butter scraped out and nothing left but the two slices of bread.

Our mailbox in Battle Creek was a big basket, which hung outside on the wall next to the front door. There were two silver hooks that held it up, and whenever we had letters to mail, we stuck the envelopes behind the tips of those hooks so the mailman would see them. At Wondrous Acres there was a honeycomb of identical mailboxes for all the trailers out on the road. You had to walk down the gravel driveway to get there. But I didn't go that way. I always cut through the weeds, angled down the hill, and walked along the ditch same as when I got off the bus, only in reverse.

That day, after we heard the horn honk, Marge sent me down to get the mail. When I got there, Audrey Krouch was standing in front of the mailboxes with a bunch of envelopes in her hand. What was weird was I almost got the feeling she'd been waiting for me.

"Hey," she said.

"Hey, yourself," I said, walking past her to get to our mailbox.

"Can I ask you a question?" she asked.

I shrugged. She could ask, but that didn't mean I was going to answer.

"How come you're afraid to walk on the driveway?" she said.

I felt my palms go slick. I hadn't expected that question. I reached into the mailbox and pulled out the mail, making a big point of sorting through it, as if I were looking for something important. Keeping my eyes down, I tried to walk past her, but she stepped right in front of me and stood there with her arms crossed, blocking my way.

"Don't pretend you didn't hear me," Audrey said. "I asked you a question. How come you're afraid to walk on the driveway?"

"Who says I am?" I said.

"I do," she said, pushing up her big glasses with a thumb. "I mean, I guess you don't *have* to walk on the driveway if you don't want to. It doesn't necessarily mean you're afraid, right?"

I shrugged.

"You could be looking for garter snakes or maybe you don't want to get gravel in your shoes, right?"

I shrugged again. If Audrey Krouch wanted to stand there all day answering her own questions, it was okay with me.

"I guess those are some pretty good reasons why you might not walk on the driveway," she said, "and I guarantee you I could come up with a bunch more just as good as those if I had to, but I don't have to because I happen to know the reason you don't want to walk on the driveway is that you're scared to."

I tasted butterscotch and swallowed. Audrey was watching me carefully. She pushed her glasses up again.

"I think you should know I have ESP," she told me solemnly.

The last thing I needed was Audrey Krouch sniffing around in my business. I pushed past her and started back down the road along the ditch. But just as I was about to cut into the weeds, she called after me, "Wait. It's not the driveway, is it? It's the office. That's what you're scared of. *The office.*"

My heart gave one hard thud in my chest. Then I whirled around and shouted at her, "You shut up, Audrey Krouch. You don't know what you're talking about. Do you hear me? You don't know squirt."

But apparently she did.

∴ 6

"WHAT DAY IS IT?" SAPPHY ASKED WHEN SHE SAW me walk in with the mail.

"Still Monday," Marge said, rolling her eyes and turning a page in her magazine.

"Coupons!" Sapphy said happily.

I was still pretty shaken up from my conversation with Audrey. It was one thing to notice that I didn't like to use the driveway—that would be pretty obvious to anybody who bothered to pay attention—but how could she possibly know about the office? Nobody knew about that. I dropped the mail on the counter, pulled the coupons out of the pile, and brought them over to where Sapphy was sitting at the table, eating orange sherbert out of her china gravy boat. That's what they called it in Michigan: sher*bert*, not sher*bet*, and with or without the extra *r*, Sapphy ate a lot of it.

When we first moved into the trailer, my mother was surprised to find that Sapphy was keeping the good bone china in her cupboard for everyday use. We'd never used ours. It was still in the box it had been sent to us in after Grandma Jeanne died. When Sapphy came home from the hospital, it didn't occur to my mother to move the china; it wasn't until after Sapphy had dropped one of the bowls and broken it that my mother decided it might be a good idea to pack up the china and put it away until Sapphy was feeling a little more coordinated. The problem was, Sapphy kept opening the cupboard expecting to find her mother's china there, and each time she didn't, she'd get upset and think that it had been stolen. Finally my mother gave up and put the china back in the cupboard. After that, Sapphy managed to break all her dishes one by one until the only thing left was the gravy boat. From then on, whenever Sapphy went looking for one of her dishes to have sherbert in, we'd give her the gravy boat and explain that it was the only thing clean at the moment. She'd laugh and say, "Well, I guess there's no law that says a person can't eat sherbert out of a gravy boat if she wants to."

I left Sapphy in the kitchen eating her sherbert

and looking over the new coupons, and I got back to my homework. Pretty soon Marge came out with her jacket on and her purse slung over her shoulder. "That wash will be ready to go in the dryer in another fifteen minutes, and then you've got to remember to take it out half an hour after that. Don't leave it sitting in the dryer or it'll wrinkle. You hear?"

I heard her, but I wouldn't be going to the laundry shed in fifteen minutes. I knew Old Gray swept the shed out last thing every afternoon before he knocked off for the day, and I wasn't about to risk running into him.

After Marge left, I went over my math, checking all my answers twice before moving on to the spelling words for the week. A little while later I heard my mother get up and start to take a shower. She didn't sing in the shower the way my father used to. He'd bellow at the top of his lungs. The morning of the day he left, I remember hearing him in the shower singing a country-western song about playing poker with a deck of fifty-one cards.

I heard the water go off, and a few minutes later my mother came out with her head wrapped up in a towel like a turban, a menthol Kool dangling from her lower lip. She squinted to keep the smoke out of her eyes.

"Marge gone?" she asked.

"Who's Marge?" said Sapphy.

My mother took the cigarette out of her mouth, bent down, and kissed Sapphy's forehead.

"Marge is your nurse, Sapph," she explained patiently. "She comes and takes care of you because you had an accident at the factory."

"Is that what happened to my hair?" asked Sapphy, reaching up and touching the uneven tufts of stiff hair that stuck up like patches of crabgrass all over her head. "I swear it wasn't like this when I went to work this morning. I look like I stuck my pinkie in a socket."

Sapphy was always the funniest of the "gem sisters." After the accident she still said funny things, but it wasn't the same. She wasn't the same. Her eyes didn't sparkle; they were flat and dull, like the eyes of the bluegills my father and I brought home from the pond on the stringer. And when I talked, even though she still listened, she didn't tilt her head to the side like a crow anymore. She couldn't really hear me, at least not the way she used to.

My mom opened the fridge, pulled out the bottom drawer with her foot, and took out a head of pale-green iceberg lettuce. Resting her burning cigarette on the edge of the sink, she tore the lettuce up and threw it in a bowl, poured bottled dressing over it, then boiled a pot of water to make macaroni and cheese. My mother used to cook real dinners back in Battle Creek. The house would start smelling good around four o'clock in the afternoon, and when suppertime rolled around at six, there'd be pot roast or pork chops or a platter of spaghetti and meatballs sitting on the table, sending up a cloud of steam. My mom always served up my dad's plate first, and sometimes he'd be ready for seconds before she'd even had a chance to serve herself. He loved her cooking, and so did I. I wondered sometimes about that cashier from the MicroMart he ran off with and whether she knew how to make meatballs or pot roast with browned potatoes and real gravy. I wondered too if while they ate their dinners together, he'd told her about me.

The kitchen at Wondrous Acres was so small, you couldn't get to the sink if the refrigerator door was open. There was a small square Formica table tucked into the corner next to the doorway.

That's where the three of us sat later that night, eating macaroni swimming in melted Velveeta cheese.

"How was your day today?" my mother asked me. She had taken the towel off her head and brushed out the tangles, but her hair was still wet and smelled fruity, like ripe peaches.

I was pushing my fork through the macaroni, attempting to maneuver a single noodle onto each one of the tines without using my fingers. I could have told her about the kids laughing at me at the bus stop and Larry Baywood threatening to squeeze my cheeks. I could have told her about Miss Miller giving me the fisheye because some guy named Arthur was coming to visit our class in the morning and she wanted us to dress up for him. Or I could have told her that Audrey Krouch claimed she had ESP. But I was afraid to tell her anything. Afraid that once I started talking, I wouldn't be able to stop until I'd told her everything, including what had happened to me on Christmas Eve in Old Gray's office. I didn't want to tell her about that. I didn't want to have to see the look on her face when she found out how dumb I had been. So I shrugged and lifted the forkful of noodles to my mouth and said nothing.

My mother sighed, crumpled her napkin in a ball, and dropped it onto her empty plate.

Suddenly I remembered the laundry.

"Be right back!" I said, jumping up from the table.

"Hold on a second, cowboy. Where do you think you're going without clearing your place?" my mother said, grabbing my arm.

"Sorry. Marge told me to put the laundry in the dryer," I said. My mother let go of me, and I picked up my dishes and carried them over to the sink.

"Take your aunt with you. She could use the fresh air, and I have to get ready for work," my mother said.

The laundry shed was an unpainted plywood barn wedged in between units 9 and 10. Inside were a couple of washers and dryers, a soap dispenser, a pop machine, and a long table for folding clothes. On the wall over the table was a big bulletin board covered with notices about church dinners, garage sales, penny socials, and used outboard motors for sale.

Sapphy, still in her pajamas and robe, stood

looking at the bulletin board while I pulled the wet clothes out of the washer, threw them into the dryer, slammed the door, and set the dial to high. As I fished some change out of my pocket, I heard her murmur, "Somebody sure pulled out all the stops for this one."

I dropped the coins into the slot and walked over to see what she was talking about. It was a flyer printed in black ink on light-blue paper, and all around the edges someone had carefully glued on dozens of silver foil stars. I knew it was those sparkly stars that had caught Sapphy's eye.

"What are they selling?" I asked, leaning closer to read the words.

★★★★★★★★★★★★★★★★★★★★★★★★★★★★

**LET MADAME YERDUA
SOLVE YOUR PROBLEMS**

**100% AUTHENTIC
PROFESSIONAL HYPNOSIS**

**NO PROBLEM TOO BIG
OR TOO SMALL**

100% FREE

★★★★★★★★★★★★★★★★★★★★★★★★★★★★

"My father did that once," said Sapphy.

"Did what?" I asked.

"Got hypnotized."

"*He did?*" I was surprised. I'd heard a lot of stories about the past, most of them more than once, but I'd never heard anything about Grandpa Will getting hypnotized.

"It was at a county fair. Your mother and Aunt Emmy had the chicken pox, so Mom stayed home to take care of them while my dad and I went to the fair. I wanted to go on the big Ferris wheel, but he didn't like heights, so instead we paid a buck apiece to go into a musty old tent where there was a man in a turban who claimed he could hypnotize people and make them bark like dogs."

"Grandpa Will let him do that to him?" I asked.

"He volunteered," she said.

My grandpa Will was a very serious man. He wore long-sleeved shirts buttoned all the way up to the top, even in the summer. He never smiled, and he always shook my hand instead of hugging me hello, even when I was really little.

"Did Grandpa Will bark?" I asked incredulously.

Sapphy grinned and nodded.

"*Really?*"

"He howled like a hound dog in front of every-body. I'll never forget it."

"Then what happened?"

"The man in the turban snapped his fingers, my father woke up, and he didn't remember a thing that had happened," Sapphy said.

"He didn't remember?"

"Not a blessed thing."

"Why not?" I asked, and now I was hanging on her every word like dew on a blade of grass.

"I don't know. I guess he must have said some-thing to make Dad forget."

"What did he say?" I asked.

Sapphy shrugged.

"I don't remember, or maybe I was too far away to hear it, but whatever it was, it sure worked. I'm telling you he *howled*, and afterward he swore up and down that he couldn't remember a thing about it."

Underneath, along the bottom of the blue flyer, the paper had been carefully cut into a fringe of even half-inch strips. On each strip was a phone number neatly printed sideways. My hands were shaking as I reached up and tore off one of the strips.

"Come on, Sapphy," I said. "It's time to go home."

7 :: ∶

MY MOTHER, DRESSED IN HER WORK CLOTHES, HER
hair dry and pulled back in a ponytail, was squat-
ting in front of the open fridge, rummaging around
on the bottom shelf when we walked in.

"What happened to all my diet cola?" she asked.
"You're not drinking it, are you, Jamie? I've told you
a million times, chemicals will stunt your growth."

I shook my head. "It's not me, it's Marge," I
told her. "But if you ask me, it doesn't look like it's
stunting her growth any."

"Don't be a wiseacre," she said. "We're lucky to
have Marge. I don't see anybody else stepping up
to help out, do you? Certainly not your good-for-
nothing—"

She didn't finish the sentence. She didn't have
to. We both knew she was talking about my dad.
I looked at her face, at the way her mouth was

pulled tight and thin, and I wondered if she remembered how she and my dad used to sit out on the porch together after dinner, talking and laughing and sometimes even kissing when they didn't think I was watching. Normal as cornflakes.

I slid my hand into my pocket and felt around for the little slip of paper. What had her name been? Madame Yerdu? Or was it Yerda? Oh, who cared what her name was? The only thing that mattered was if she knew the magic words. I knew nothing could ever undo what had happened, but maybe just maybe I would finally be able to forget. I felt antsy as I watched my mother digging around in the fridge. *Hurry up and go*, I thought. *Hurry up and go.*

Finally she managed to find a lone can of diet cola hiding way in the back, pulled it out, and stuck it in her purse. She'd drink it on one of her breaks, to help keep her awake until her shift was over.

"Sapph, do you want any more macaroni before I soak the pot?" my mother said.

"Did we eat already?" Sapphy asked.

Mom sighed.

"Yes, Sapph. We just ate," she said.

"Funny, I don't remember that," Sapphy said.

"I'm not hungry, though. Except maybe for some sherbert."

My mom scraped the last of the macaroni into a Tupperware bowl and stuck it in the fridge. Then she squirted dish detergent into the pot and set it to soak in the sink.

"Give your aunt some sherbert while I get her sleeping pill," she told me.

Sapphy was standing in front of the open cupboard, looking forlornly at the old blue-and-white dishes we'd brought with us from Battle Creek.

"What in the world are these doing in here?" she asked. "These aren't my dishes. Where's my good china?"

My mom came back with Sapphy's pill.

"Here you go," she said, handing it to her along with a glass of water. "Take this, and you'll be set till the morning, when Marge comes."

"Who's Marge?" Sapphy asked.

My mother looked at me and shook her head.

"Sometimes I'm tempted to take one of these pills myself," she said.

She pulled a crumpled pack of Kools out of her pocket, lit one, blew smoke out the side of her mouth, and kissed me on the cheek. Smoke and peaches mixed, like burned cobbler.

"Don't forget to do magic triggers tonight," she told me as she put on her coat. "Oh, and I keep forgetting to tell you, I found something new I think might be worth trying."

"What is it?" I asked.

"A formal."

"What's that?" I said.

"A dress. It's long and blue—you can't miss it. It's hanging in the back of the closet in her room in a dry cleaner's bag. She loved that dress, and you never know, maybe it will trigger something."

One of the doctors Sapphy saw after her accident told us that sometimes a person with amnesia can get her memory back all of a sudden if the right thing triggers it. The magic trigger could be anything—a photograph or a song or the smell of a cherry pie baking in the oven. Sapphy's memories were like keys jangling on a big ring, and it was up to us to keep trying them until we found the one that would finally pop the lock.

We decided to look for magic triggers room by room, starting with the kitchen. One of the first things we tried was the spice rack that hung on the wall next to the stove. We opened up all the little bottles and cans, letting Sapphy sniff the powders and dried-up leaves inside each one. My mother had kept her spices jammed in a little cupboard over the stove in Battle Creek, but Sapphy's were lined up in the rack, alphabetized with the labels facing out. Allspice, Basil, Bay Leaf, Cardamom, Cinnamon, Coriander, Curry. When we got to Nutmeg, I pried open the lid and was instantly reminded of the eggnog my father used to make on New Year's Eve, when my parents would have a few of the neighbors over to ring in the new year. He always ladled out a cup for me before he poured in the booze. Virgin Nog, he called it.

After the spices, we moved on to the refrigerator, opening all the bottles and jars of condiments in the door. Sapphy tasted steak sauce and mustard, maraschino cherries, and sweet pickle relish, but none turned out to be a magic trigger.

When we'd exhausted all the trigger possibilities in the kitchen, we turned our attention to the old-fashioned record player out in the living room.

"Maybe Sapphy's trigger is a song," my mother said. "She's always loved music."

I knew the names of the Motown groups I listened to in the morning on the radio, but Sapphy's record collection was full of people I'd never heard of. Like the spice rack, they were kept in alphabetical order, so we started at the beginning and made our way through them, one album at a time. We listened to Rosemary Clooney, Tommy Dorsey, Peggy Lee, Glenn Miller, and, when we hit the *S*'s, Frank Sinatra. Sapphy had more Sinatra than anything else, and each time we put him on, she would say the same thing: "Nobody sings like Old Blue Eyes. Boy, does this take me back."

The trouble was Sapphy didn't need to go back. She needed to go forward, but like I said before, she was a lot like one of those records. They were scratched, and the needle would get stuck and keep repeating the same line over and over until I stamped my foot hard on the floor and it jumped the scratch and kept playing. But nothing we came up with seemed to be able to trigger Sapphy's memory and help her jump the scratch.

At first those Sinatra songs seemed painfully corny, but after a while I began to understand what Sapphy meant when she said nobody sang like Old Blue Eyes. It was true—nobody did, and some of those songs, especially the one called "Mood Indigo," really got to me. Sometimes I'd put it on even when Sapphy wasn't around.

My least favorite trigger hunt was probably Sapphy's favorite—going through the family photo album. There was an endless number of pictures in there of the "gem sisters" when they were little. She'd point to the faded black-and-white snapshots, explaining that she had been the little girl with the dark hair, and my mother, Opal, had the light, and Emmy wore glasses and had curls. But the main reason I dreaded looking at the family album was that on a page near the end there was a picture of my mom and dad on their wedding day. My dad was wearing a dark suit and had his hair slicked back. My mom had a little wreath of roses in her hair and her arm tight around my dad's waist, pulling him in close to her. They looked so happy, it made me ache just like that Frank Sinatra song.

"So you'll try the dress with her, right, Jamie?" my mother said.

I shrugged, then nodded.

"Promise?" she said.

"Promise," I said, slipping my hand into my pocket once more to check for the little slip of paper.

Hurry up and go. Hurry up and go.

It seemed like it took forever before I finally heard the car start up and the crunch of gravel as my mother pulled out and headed off to work. I knew that I should go look for that dress she'd mentioned or at least put on a record. I had promised my mother that I would do triggers, and I knew from experience that it had to be done before Sapphy's pill kicked in or there wouldn't be any point. But I had been waiting such a long time, I didn't think I could wait another minute. I pulled the slip of blue paper out of my pocket, reached for the phone, and dialed.

8 ∴

"WHO ARE YOU CALLING?" SAPPHY ASKED.

"Shhh!" I said, putting a finger to my lips. *One ring.*

She pulled open the cupboard. "Where the heck are my dishes?" she muttered.

Two rings.

I'd forgotten I was supposed to get her some sherbert. I reached over and grabbed the gravy boat out of the dish drainer and held it out to Sapphy.

Three.

"This is the only thing that's clean, Sapph," I said.

"Sherbert in a gravy boat?" She laughed. "Whoever heard of such a thing?"

Four rings.

Shaking her head, she took it from me and carried it over to the table. "I guess there's no law that says a person can't eat sherbert out of a gravy boat if she wants to."

Five —

"Hello?"

Sapphy was banging around, looking for a spoon in the drawer, making it hard for me to hear. I turned away from her, putting my finger in one ear and pressing the receiver harder into the other.

"Uh, hello. My name is Jamie Reardon, and I'm calling about getting hypnotized," I said. "Is this Madame . . . Yerda?"

"It's Yerdua," she corrected. "Yer-du-ah. And I'd be glad to hypnotize you. When do you want to do it?"

In the short amount of time that had passed between when I'd first torn the little slip of paper off the flyer and when I'd dialed the number written on it, I had formed a picture of what I thought Madame Yerdua would be like. I expected with a name like hers that she would have an accent and a deep, mysterious-sounding voice. I imagined that she would hypnotize me in a tent, like the one Sapphy had described at the county fair. She might wear a turban too, or at the very least big hoop earrings and a scarf on her head. What I had not expected was that I would recognize her voice on the other end of the line, and it would make my blood boil.

"Audrey Krouch, is that you?" I said.

"My professional name is Madame Yerdua," she told me.

"Cut it out, Audrey. I know it's you," I said. "And I don't think it's funny."

"What are you yelling for?" Audrey said. "I didn't tell you to call me up, did I?"

"You've got a lot of nerve hanging up that flyer," I said.

"It's a free country. I'm allowed to advertise if I want to."

"Not when it's a bunch of lies, you're not," I said. "You don't know how to hypnotize anybody, and your name's not Madame Yerdua either."

"Yerdua is Audrey backward, so it's still my name, and I do so know how to hypnotize people. I'll come over there right now and prove it if you don't believe me."

All of a sudden there was a loud crash. It startled me so much that I jumped and dropped the phone. Sapphy had knocked the gravy boat off the table, and it lay in pieces on the floor, orange sherbert puddled in the middle, splattered on her slippers and up her pale, bare legs.

"Oh, no," she wailed.

"Are you okay, Sapph?" I asked anxiously. "Did you cut yourself?"

Tears began to stream down her cheeks.

"Look what I did. I broke Mom's gravy boat."

I grabbed the phone by the cord and pulled up the receiver like a fish on a line. "You better not tell anybody I called you, Audrey Krouch," I shouted into it. "Audrey?" But she was gone. The line was dead, along with my ridiculous hope that some mysterious stranger in a turban was going to be able to solve my problems. For free no less. What a chump. I hung up the phone and turned my attention back to Sapphy.

"It's okay," I said, getting down on my hands and knees and beginning to clean up the mess. "Don't cry, Sapph. It was just an accident."

As I began to pick up the broken pieces of china, I realized how absurd it was for me to be feeling jealous of poor Sapphy standing there in her ratty old robe and sherbert-splattered slippers, crying over a broken gravy boat. But I couldn't help it. I was. In a little while she'd be sound asleep in her bed, and I'd be out in the living room surrounded by empty cherry cans, too afraid to close my eyes. And what's more, in the morning, when she woke up, she wouldn't remember a thing about what had happened.

I could tell Sapphy's sleeping pill was beginning to work, but I went to her room and got the dress out of the closet anyway.

"What in the world are you doing with that?" she asked when I came back into the room with the dress draped over my arm.

"Come sit with me on the couch," I told her.

I held Sapphy's arm by the elbow to keep her steady, and we walked over and sat down on the couch.

"My mother made this for me," she said, as I pulled the thin plastic bag over the top of the hanger and laid the long midnight-blue dress across our knees.

"I didn't know Grandma Jeanne sewed."

"Oh, she was very good. She could do just about anything with that old Singer of hers. She made all our clothes for us when we were little. Beautiful little dresses, with sashes and smocking."

"You weren't little when she made this dress, though," I said.

"No. I was sixteen. It was for a wedding."

"Whose wedding?"

"Barb Shaw."

"Who's that?"

"Just a girl we knew who got married," Sapphy said. "Our whole family was invited to the ceremony, and then afterward there was a reception at the Westerner Buffet Restaurant. I remember the shrimp. Great big fat ones. Her parents were both doctors, so they could afford that kind of thing. There was cocktail sauce too, with horseradish in it."

"I don't like horseradish," I said.

"You might when you're older. It grows on you. Like coffee."

"What's this made out of, anyway?" I asked, rubbing the plush blue fabric between my thumb and finger.

"Velveteen," she said, "like the rabbit in that old story."

"It's soft," I said.

"Mm-hmm," said Sapphy as she ran her hand slowly down the front of the dress. Then she closed her eyes and stroked it in the other direction, against the nap, her fingers leaving little trails as they went. "My mother made all the buttonholes by hand, and she covered the buttons with fabric so they'd match perfectly. I stood on one of our dining room chairs while she pinned up the hem. I remember she couldn't talk because she had pins sticking out of her mouth. She looked like a—like a—"

"Porcupine?" I said.

Sapphy smiled and sighed deeply as her chin dropped down to her chest. The pill had finally kicked in. I helped her up and managed to get her into bed. Then I slipped the blue dress back into the plastic bag and hung it up in the closet. Yet another key that hadn't fit the lock.

As I switched off the light and pulled Sapphy's door closed, for the second time that night I suddenly remembered the laundry. I was not supposed to leave Sapphy alone in the house, but if Marge arrived in the morning and found out that despite her warning, I had left the clothes sitting in the dryer overnight, I'd never hear the end of it. I was sure Sapphy wouldn't wake up, not that soon after the pill had kicked in, so I pulled on my jacket and quickly ran down to the laundry shed. A minute later I was leaning against the dryer, waiting to catch my breath, when I heard a noise at the door and turned around to find Audrey Krouch standing there.

"Hey," she said. "What are you doing here so late?"

"It's a free country," I said sarcastically.

I opened the door of the dryer and pulled out a wad of wrinkled clothes.

"I hope you have an iron," Audrey said.

I gave her a dirty look.

"I don't know what your problem is. It's not my fault you called me up tonight," she said.

"Yes, it is," I said. Then I went over to the bulletin board, tore the light-blue flyer off the board, and ripped it in half. A couple of silver stars came loose and fluttered down to the floor.

"I can just make another one," she said with a shrug. "I've got a whole box of those stars."

"You better not make another one," I said, "or I'll rip that one down too."

"You're just jealous because I have special powers."

"That's the dumbest thing I ever heard," I scoffed. "You don't have any special powers."

"I do so. I told you, I have ESP," she said, pushing up her glasses, "Extrasensory perception. I can see things nobody else can see."

"Must be your glasses," I said.

"For your information, these glasses *do* help me see," she said.

"Oh, come on. They don't even have glass in them," I said. "How could they help you see?"

"It's not that kind of seeing," she said.

"What other kind is there?"

"The kind that lets me read someone's mind," she said.

"Give me a break," I told her. "You can't read minds, Audrey. And you don't have ESP either."

"Oh, yeah? Then how come I know you're scared of the office?" she asked.

"I told you, you don't know squirt," I said.

"I suppose I don't know squirt about cherry cans either, then, huh?"

A chill went right up my spine and made me shiver so hard, I bit my tongue. "Ouch!" I said, tasting blood.

"The reason I'm so good at hypnotizing people is because I have ESP. It helps if you can read their minds first." Audrey looked at me and pushed up her glasses. "You thirsty?" she asked.

"I thought you said you could read my mind," I said.

"I can," she told me. "I was just being polite."

Then she walked over to the pop machine and gave it a good swift kick in the side. There was a deep rumbling from within, and a second later an ice-cold bottle of orange Faygo rolled out.

"Hey!" I said in amazement.

"Hey, yourself," she said, and did it again.

She handed me one of the bottles. I twisted off the cap and took a long swallow.

"See, I knew you were thirsty," she said.

"I just like orange pop is all," I told her, but I was beginning to wonder if I had misjudged Audrey Krouch.

9 ⠒⠂

I'M NOT SURE EXACTLY HOW AUDREY MANAGED TO convince me that I should go over to her house and let her try to hypnotize me the next day after school, but she did.

"Okay. See you tomorrow," she said as we left the laundry shed after we'd finished our orange pop and I'd done my best to fold up the wrinkled laundry.

⠒

The next morning at the bus stop Audrey looked different. Her hair, which was usually uncombed and snarled in the morning, was pulled back in a tight ponytail, and instead of her usual jeans and T-shirt she was wearing a dress. You could tell it was new because the skirt stuck out stiffly, and she kept scratching her neck as if the collar were itching her. Of course she had her glasses on, and with her hair pulled back that way, her head looked smaller, which made the glasses seem even bigger and more ridiculous than usual.

"Hey," she said.

"Hey, yourself. So what's with the dress?"

"We're supposed to dress up today, remember?" she said.

I hadn't remembered. But it wouldn't have made any difference anyway. I did a quick survey of what I was wearing and was relieved to find that at least everything was clean.

"So you're coming over this afternoon, right?" she said.

I looked around nervously at the other kids waiting for the bus, hoping nobody had heard what she'd just said.

"I guess," I said quietly.

"Well, don't be too enthusiastic about it or anything," she told me. "I'm doing you a favor, you know. People pay hundreds of dollars to get hypnotized. Sometimes thousands."

"My grandfather only paid a buck," I told her.

"Your grandfather got hypnotized?" Audrey asked, pushing her glasses up and leaning toward me with interest.

"Yeah, at a county fair."

"Oh. Well, it probably wasn't a professional then, just some clown in a turban."

"Are you going to wear a turban when you do it?" I asked.

She snorted and pulled at her collar. "Of course not. That's hokey."

"Are you going to wear that dress?"

"Are you kidding? This thing is giving me hives. I'm bumping up, see?"

She pulled the collar of the dress to one side and showed me her neck, which was red and blotchy.

The bus came then, and we got on.

"Hey, Rear-end," Larry said, grinning at me as I walked past. "How's your crack?"

I looked down and didn't say anything, but Audrey, who was walking in front of me, suddenly whirled around and snapped, "Can't you think of anything else to say? That crack thing is getting so old, it's got wrinkles."

Larry was speechless, and so was I. Nobody ever talked back to him.

"Are you nuts?" I whispered as I followed her down the aisle. When we reached the back of the bus, I quickly slid into my usual seat. Instead of taking one of the open seats around me, Audrey slid in next to me.

"Hey, what are you doing?" I said. "You can't sit here."

"It's a free country," she said, leaning back and crossing her arms, "I can sit anywhere I want."

I began to sweat. It didn't take a genius to know this was not going to go unnoticed.

"Oh, I get it now," Larry said loudly, hanging over the back of his seat and pointing at us. "Look, everybody. Rear-end got himself a girlfriend to stick up for him. Are you going to smooch her? Come on, Rear-end, give her a big wet smooch right on the mouth, why don't ya?"

Everybody turned around to look and laugh.

"*Move,*" I whispered fiercely.

But Audrey grabbed two handfuls of stiff skirt, jammed it under her legs, put one foot up on the back of the seat in front of her, and didn't budge.

I guess hearing everybody laughing like that was enough to make Larry feel that he'd evened the score. He quit razzing me and went back to talking with his friends.

A couple of minutes later we crossed over the

railroad tracks. As the bus lurched, Audrey fell against me.

"Watch it," I said, pushing her off and pressing up against the side of the bus as far away from her as possible.

"Jeez Louise. What are you so touchy about? I don't bite, you know."

I wasn't about to tell her that besides being afraid to walk up my own driveway or close my eyes at night, I also had a hard time being touched.

"Just watch it, okay?" I told her.

When we got to school, Miss Miller was all dressed up with her lips painted even redder than usual. She had a pink silk scarf with red hearts tied around her neck, and as she walked around the room, the ends fluttered like the little triangular colored flags you see at used-car lots. She wore high heels. Those shoes didn't just make Miss Miller taller; they made her walk in a whole new way. I was slumped over my desk, staring at the pattern in one of the linoleum floor tiles, when Arthur arrived.

"James!" Miss Miller's voice cut clean through me like piano wire through a stick of cold butter. "Sit up like a gentleman. Where are your manners?

We've got company!"

She rushed over to him, her scarf flapping, her high heels clicking on the polished floor. Blushing, he reached out and shook hands with her. He was tall and thin, with a long neck and a giant Adam's apple that slid up and down above his collar like an elevator when he swallowed. His hair was reddish brown and curly, and he wore tiny round wire glasses that looked so much like part of his face, he might have been born wearing them.

"We're just *thrilled* that you could come!" she gushed. "I can't begin to tell you how honored we are to have you as our guest."

Arthur smiled and said something back, but it was too soft for me to hear. Miss Miller took his coat and hung it in her special closet. Then her red mouth started going again, telling Arthur how excited she was and squeezing his arm the whole time she was talking. His cheeks were getting pink, as if the pressure of her fingers were rerouting all the blood up into his face. The more she talked, the pinker he got. Finally she stopped to catch her breath, and I realized I'd been holding mine the whole time. Even in those high-heeled shoes of hers, she was quite a bit shorter than he was, but the way she was looking up at him, it seemed like any second she might leap up and swallow him whole.

"It's very nice to meet you all," Arthur said, turning his attention and his pink face to us. "And I'm grateful to the PTA for helping to bring me here to Pine Tree Elementary."

His voice was soft and scratchy, and he seemed kind of nervous. I'd have been nervous too, standing that close to Miss Miller. I leaned back in my chair and slid my thumbs over my ears. Open closed, open closed. Word slaw. I must have shut my eyes.

"*James Reardon!*" Miss Miller shouted, clapping her hands right next to my head, startling me so badly, I actually jumped up out of my seat, banging my knee painfully against the sharp edge of the desk. "Have you heard one word that's been said?"

"Yes, ma'am. I heard everything," I lied, rubbing my knee as I felt the color rise hot in my own cheeks.

"Good," she said. "Then you won't mind repeating it for us, will you?"

She stared bug-eyed at me, waiting for my response.

"Um . . . you were saying that you're so thrilled that Arthur, um, that it's an honor that Arthur—" I began.

"Excuse me," Miss Miller said, her lips quivering with emotion. "Whom, may I ask, are you referring to as *Arthur*?"

I slowly raised my arm and pointed at Arthur, who was standing right there next to her, looking pinker and more uncomfortable than ever.

The whole class erupted in raucous laughter.

"Who would like to explain to James his embarrassing mistake? Who would like to tell him who our guest this morning really is?" Miss Miller said, looking around. "Yes, Mary Lynne?"

Of course it would be Mary Lynne. Miss Miller's class pet stood up, her round face contorted in a junior version of the same contempt Miss Miller was just barely managing to contain herself. She was dressed in her Sunday best, her white-blond hair curled in ringlets and pulled back with a shiny blue ribbon.

"Our guest this morning is Mr. Anthony Stone," she said. "He is a published author who lives in Traverse City, and he has come to talk to all the fifth grades about how to become better writers."

"Thank you, dear," said Miss Miller, before turning back to me. "*Author*, not *Arthur*," she said. "Mr. Stone is our *visiting author*."

I wanted to cry, or scream, or beat my fists against the wall, I was so humiliated. I wanted to run out the door and keep on running, all the way back to Battle Creek. Instead I sat there pretending not to care, tasting butterscotch, and feeling the button pressing into my cheek. It had left a mark. Four round, raised bumps inside a perfect little pink circle. A reminder that no matter what, you don't ever let anybody know how you feel.

∴ 10

AFTER THE LAUGHTER AND JOKING DIED DOWN, WE were told to go over to the meeting rug and sit cross-legged with clipboards and pencils in our laps. I took my usual spot in the corner as far away from everyone else as I could get and still be technically on the rug. I hated rug time. People sat so close, you could smell the soap on their skin and whether or not they'd brushed their teeth that morning. Knees and elbows were always bumping into me, and I worried about the rug's not being clean.

Audrey Krouch plopped down next to me in her stiff dress, the back of her neck streaked with red where she'd been scratching herself. Arthur—I never called him that out loud again, but he will always be Arthur to me—stood uncomfortably before us and started to teach.

"Does anybody know what descriptive writing is?" he began.

His voice was so soft, it was hard to understand what he was saying unless you kept your eyes on his lips the whole time he was talking.

Mary Lynne raised her hand with the usual accompanying sharp gasp to indicate how eager she was to be called on.

"Descriptive writing is writing that describes something," she said, flashing a triumphant smile first at Arthur and then at Miss Miller, who was sitting on a chair at the edge of the rug with her own pencil poised over a clipboard, nodding approvingly.

"Show-off," Audrey muttered under her breath. Then she leaned closer to me and whispered, "She's got a big wart on her finger. Did you ever see it? *Disgusting.*"

"Let's start with some examples," Arthur said.

He reached into his bag and pulled out a stack of books, which he placed on the corner of Miss Miller's desk. Slips of pink paper stuck out from between the pages like little tongues marking the passages he'd chosen to read to us. I hated read aloud. Miss Miller always picked boring books, and she'd make up squeaky little voices for each character in the story, which made listening to her read unbearable. I leaned forward, putting my elbows on my knees and resting my chin on my fists, thumbs out and ready to slip over my ears the minute I needed to escape.

"Anybody here ever read *Old Yeller*?" Arthur asked.

I had—twice, actually—but I didn't raise my hand. I never did.

Arthur opened the book to one of the paper tongues near the beginning and began to read a passage describing the boy, Travis, building a split-rail fence. It wasn't the part I would have chosen to read. The best part of the book comes later, after Yeller fights with the mad wolf and gets rabies, but at least Arthur's voice didn't irritate me the way Miss Miller's did. He read everything in a normal tone, with no squeaky character voices.

"I've never built a fence in my life," he said when he had finished reading and laid the book down, "but I almost feel as though I could after reading that, don't you?"

The next book he read from was another one of my favorites, *My Side of the Mountain*. It's all about this boy, Sam, who goes off to live in the woods on his own. The part he read was a description of how Sam scrapes the flesh off a deer hide and chews and rubs it to make it soft and pliable enough to serve as a door for the hollowed-out tree he lives in.

Mary Lynne raised her hand right in the middle of it and waved it around so much, Arthur had no choice but to stop reading and call on her.

"Wouldn't it be dangerous to chew on an animal's skin without cooking it first?" she asked. "My mother says you can die from touching raw chicken."

"I wouldn't worry about it," said Arthur with a little smile. "I've read this book a dozen times, and Sam always comes through it just fine."

Finally, he read us a chapter from a book that he had written himself called *Losing Perfect*. It was about a kid who gets up one morning and comes downstairs to find that there's nobody home. At first he thinks his parents are probably out taking a walk or something, but when he goes to look for them, he finds that all the other houses in the neighborhood are empty too. There are no kids riding bikes in the street, no dogs in the yards, or birds in the trees. There's nobody left in the world but him.

As Arthur read to us, his soft voice wrapped itself around each word like the tissue paper we used and reused each year to wrap up the Christmas ornaments and keep them from bumping against each other in the boxes when we put them away at the end of the season. We had always made such a big deal out of Christmas in Battle Creek. It was my favorite time of year. Considering everything that had happened that year, though, I guess I shouldn't have been surprised when my mother told me we weren't going to have a tree at Wondrous Acres.

"What have we got to celebrate?" she said.

Maybe if I had begged her for a tree instead of just sulking about it, she might have changed her mind. We would have gone out together and picked out a nice big fat one and brought it home strapped to the roof of the car the way we always had before. She would have made hot chocolate and sugar cookies shaped like bells and holly leaves, and we would have carefully unwrapped all the ornaments and hung them one by one on the tree. If only we'd had a tree of our own to decorate, things would have been different. I wouldn't have needed to go to Old Gray's office on Christmas Eve, and if I hadn't gone there— But there was no point in going down this road again. It was too late to change what had happened. The sudden sweet taste of butterscotch flooding my mouth, as I sat there on the crowded meeting rug that day while Arthur read to us, was the only reminder I needed that school was not a safe place to be thinking about this stuff and feeling sorry for myself.

I let Arthur's voice pull me out of my own head and back into his story, and after a while I found that I no longer needed to watch his lips in order to be able to understand what he was saying. I closed my eyes and began to rock back and forth to the rhythm of the words, images from the book taking shape behind my eyelids. Suddenly a hissing noise hit my ears like spit on a hot iron, and I opened my eyes to find Miss Miller glaring down at me, fiercely mouthing something with her terrible red lips.

"Ssssit up!" she hissed. "This instant!"

I straightened up with a jerk, accidentally bumping knees hard with Audrey. Startled, I flinched instinctively, rocked over onto one hip, and shot my legs out to the side, catching her just under the ribs with my feet. She yelped and scooted quickly out of reach.

"Get off me!" I shouted. "Get away!"

Everybody turned around to stare and snicker. Miss Miller pressed her lips together and shook her head.

"As you can see, Mr. Stone, some of us are unable to behave properly when there's a guest in the room," she said. Then she turned to me. "Apologize to Mr. Stone for your rudeness, please."

"It wasn't his fault, Miss Miller," Audrey interrupted quickly. "It was mine. I squished his fingers by accident with my shoe. That's why he yelled like that. He couldn't help it."

I didn't know what to say, I was so surprised. Her foot hadn't been anywhere near my fingers.

"Fine. Then you can both apologize to Mr. Stone for the interruption," Miss Miller said.

"We're sorry," said Audrey quickly.

"Yeah," I said. "Sorry." And I was. Sorry I had

kicked Audrey, sorry I had interrupted Arthur's reading, sorry I was so pathetic that a girl had to come to my rescue.

Arthur closed the book he'd been reading and looked at me. "Okay," he said. "It's your turn."

∴ 11

I BRACED MYSELF, FIGURING HE WAS GOING TO MAKE me read something out loud in front of everyone. Miss Miller did that all the time. Made us stand up in front of the class and recite poems or do math problems on the board. Other kids didn't seem to mind it, Mary Lynne *loved* it, but for me it was excruciating to be up there in front of everyone, chalk squeaking in my sweaty hand, tripping over my own thoughts and words, terrified that somehow, as I stood there in the spotlight, they would be able to see right through me all the way to the secret I was desperately trying to hide. As it turned out, though, Arthur wasn't talking to me in particular; he was talking to the entire class.

"I'd like you each to try writing a description of your own now," he said.

A couple of kids near me groaned, but I exhaled

and gave silent thanks.

"I know," Arthur said. "It sounds hard. But trust me, it's not really."

"What would you like us to describe, Mr. Stone?" asked Miss Miller.

"I was thinking we'd start with a place," he said, "a place you have a good feeling about. It could be somewhere you went on vacation with your family, or maybe it's your grandmother's kitchen. It doesn't matter where it is, as long as it's special to you."

Pencils began scratching away before Arthur had even finished telling us what he wanted us to do.

"Hang on," said Arthur. "Before you start writing, I want to let you in on a little secret."

He went to the board and wrote:

SIGHT

SOUND

SMELL

TASTE

TOUCH

Mary Lynne gasped and shot her hand up into the air, but Arthur's back was to the class as he wrote on the board, so he couldn't see her. Finally, unable to contain herself, she blurted out, "I know! I know! Those are the five senses."

"Yes," Arthur said, putting down the chalk and turning around to face us again. "And they are your five best friends when it comes to descriptive writing. If you're writing about your grandmother's kitchen, don't just tell us what it *looks* like; use some of your other senses too. Tell us what it *smells* like when you walk into the room or what the countertop *feels* like when you run your hand over it. What *sound* do her shoes make when she walks across the floor to hug you hello? Using as many of your senses as you can will help make your writing come alive."

He gave us ten minutes to write about our special place. I spent the whole time thinking about my room back in Battle Creek.

I thought about lying in my bed in the dark, talking to Mister. In summertime at night with the windows open it smelled like . . . cut grass and charcoal from the barbecue grill. Some of the older boys from the neighborhood called out to each other, laughing as they played Capture the Flag in the moonlight. I heard the sound of my parents' voices downstairs, talking back and forth in the kitchen, water running, and the clinking of dinner dishes being washed. The warm breeze made the curtains pouf out like those skirts ballerinas wear, and crickets made the air buzz. I'd hold my fingers against Mister's throat and feel him purring steadily like the old treadle sewing machine my mother kept up in the attic. I ticked off the senses on my fingers: one, two, three, four. Which one had I left out? Oh, right: taste. If a room could taste of something, what would mine have tasted of? Chocolate pudding and cinnamon toast, blue raspberry ice pops from the Good Humor truck, and my mother's lipsticky good-night kisses when she and my father got dressed up and went out to cocktail parties and special anniversary dinners together.

"Okay. Time's up. Anybody want to volunteer to read what they wrote?" Arthur asked, looking out expectantly over the class sitting before him on the floor.

Mary Lynne was the only one with her hand up.

"How about someone we haven't heard from

yet this morning?" Arthur said, looking around.

Audrey Krouch pulled at her collar and tentatively raised her hand. She had written a description of riding in her father's car. She said that he always let her sit in the front and pick out the radio stations, and that she liked to look at the maps he kept folded up under the front seat. She said she especially liked the way it smelled like her father inside the car when you first got in. I thought it was pretty good, what she wrote, but Larry made a rude comment about how her dad must have bad BO to be able to stink up a whole car that way, and Miss Miller gave *him* the big fisheye for a change.

A few other kids read, and finally Arthur called on Mary Lynne, who looked as if she might explode if she didn't get to go next. Hers was lame. She had tried to suck up by using Arthur's idea of writing about her grandmother's kitchen, but she said the countertop felt like Formica and it sounded like shoes on the floor when her grandma ran over to hug her hello. I looked over at Audrey to see if she was having the same reaction I was, but she was still busy scowling at

Larry Baywood for what he'd said about her dad's having BO.

No matter how bad any of the descriptions were, after each person read, Arthur said something encouraging. "Nice work." "Good effort." "Interesting choice."

Once they realized they weren't going to get slammed even if what they wrote stank, they all wanted to "share," as Miss Miller insisted on calling it. Larry Baywood hammed it up when he read his, adding stuff for laughs that you could tell he hadn't really written down on the page. Miss Miller read her description too. She wrote about the classroom's being her favorite place and how she felt that the kids were like beautiful flowers growing in her garden. Arthur said he thought that was "a very nice image." I wondered what kind of flower Miss Miller imagined I was.

When everybody else had read, Arthur looked at me.

"What about it, James?" he said.

I was surprised when he called me by name. Then I realized he must have remembered Miss Miller had called me James when she yelled at me earlier. I shook my head no, and Arthur nodded as if to say it was okay with him if I didn't want to read, but Miss Miller stepped in.

"Mr. Stone has asked you to read," she said.

I could have done what Larry did, made up things that I hadn't actually written down. I could have told about the crickets and the curtains and the way it felt to lie there in the dark with Mister in my old room, but instead I shook my head again.

"I don't have anything," I said.

Miss Miller pursed her lips and rolled her eyes. "Give me your paper, James," she said, holding out her hand. I noticed for the first time that the polish on her sharp nails was the same blood red as her lips.

I pressed the heel of my hand down on the clip at the top of my board, pulled out the blank sheet of paper, and handed it to her. She looked at it, front and back.

"I do apologize, Mr. Stone," she said.

"No apology necessary," Arthur told her. "A blank page is often a sign of something promising to come."

Miss Miller laughed sharply. "I wouldn't hold my breath," she said as she crumpled my paper into a tight ball and threw it into the trash basket beside her desk.

: : 12

WE SPENT THAT WHOLE MORNING WORKING WITH Arthur. After doing the descriptions, he talked to us a little about keeping a writer's notebook.

"I take mine with me everywhere I go," he said.

"Perhaps you could give the children an idea of the kinds of things you write down in your notebook," Miss Miller said. "Ideas for new books?"

"Sure, if one happens to come to me. But mostly it's random things I hear or see. I keep a couple of running lists, too." He reached into his jacket pocket and pulled out a small black notebook. He opened it and began to flip through the pages. "Here's a list of good words to describe how people walk: stride, shuffle, limp, swagger—" He stopped and flipped through more pages. "I've got pages of beauty parlor puns, names people call their pets, strange restaurant behavior."

"Fascinating," said Miss Miller.

"I don't know about that," he said, closing the notebook and slipping it back into his pocket, "but I do think keeping a notebook handy is a good idea."

With the remaining time we had together that morning, Arthur decided to work with us on dialogue.

"Do you all know what dialogue is?" he asked.

Mary Lynne raised her hand, of course, but Arthur called on someone else, a boy named Kevin Kaminsky, who had a red birthmark on his forehead and rode the same bus I did.

"A dialogue is when two people are talking to each other," Kevin said.

Arthur nodded and went on. "I'd like you all to write down a few lines of dialogue from a conversation you can remember hearing in the past day or so. I want you to write down all the words, exactly the way you remember them, but I don't want you to tell us who's speaking," he explained.

"Can it have cusses in it?" Larry Baywood asked.

"Absolutely not." Miss Miller chimed in before

Arthur could answer the question himself.

"Should we use quotation marks?" Mary Lynne asked, shooting a quick look over at Miss Miller to see if she was pleased with the question.

"I'm more interested in the words than the punctuation, but if you want to use quotation marks, that's fine," Arthur said.

"Does spelling count?" Kevin asked.

Arthur shook his head.

"Can one of the two people talking be yourself?" someone else asked.

He nodded. "As long as you don't tell us who's talking," he said. "And don't put your names on your papers either. These are going to be anonymous dialogues."

Miss Miller came and stood right behind me. I knew why she was there. She wanted to make sure I wrote something down this time. It made me so nervous, her standing that close to me, I couldn't think about anything other than the fact that she was there. All around me pencils scratched away, but my mind was a total blank.

Someone knocked at the door, probably a message from the office or a stack of forms to be handed out at the end of the day. Miss Miller went to answer it, but before she did, she leaned over and whispered in my ear, "Don't you dare put me to shame again. Do you hear me? Don't you dare."

A few minutes later Arthur clapped his hands and asked us all to pass forward our papers. I opened the clip at the top of my board and passed the top sheet to the front along with the others.

"I'm going to read these dialogues aloud now," Arthur told us, "and then we're going to see if we can tell what kind of person is speaking, based only on the words."

It was harder than it sounded. The first dialogue went like this:

May I have something to drink, please?
What would you like to drink?
I would like some orange juice, please.

"What can you tell about the two people who are having this dialogue?" Arthur asked.

"One of them is thirsty," said Larry.

Everyone laughed, and Larry looked pleased with himself.

"Okay. But *who* is thirsty? Is it a little boy? Is it an old woman? A talking rabbit?"

"It's me," Mary Lynne called out, "and my mom. This morning at breakfast."

"Okay. So much for being anonymous." Arthur laughed. "But here's the point. If you hadn't just told us it was you and your mother having this dialogue, there's no way we would have known it just from listening to the words, would we?"

"Those are the exact words we said," Mary Lynne said defensively. "I remember perfectly. It's not my fault you wouldn't let us say who was talking."

"Let's read a few more," Arthur said, quickly moving on.

He read several more dialogues, all of which had the exact same problem. The words sounded as if anybody could have said them. When Arthur picked up the next paper in the pile, his eyebrows went up, and he smiled.

"Ah. Here we go. How about this one?" he said. "*Don't you dare put me to shame again. Do you hear me? Don't you dare.*"

"That's somebody old and mean talking," a red-headed girl named Emily said.

"How do you know?" Arthur asked.

"Because a kid wouldn't say it that way. A kid

wouldn't say, 'Don't you dare.'"

"If it was me, I'd say, 'Knock it off or I'll cream you.'" Larry agreed.

"Exactly," said Arthur. "The message says, 'Knock it off or I'll cream you,' but these particular words tell you the person who's talking is old and mean."

I was afraid to look at Miss Miller. I knew she must be furious. I hadn't meant for this to happen. I just wrote down the only thing I could think of.

Mary Lynne's hand was up again. "That's not a dialogue," she said. "There's only one person talking. You said a dialogue is two people talking."

"The point is that by using these particular words, this writer was able to tell us—"

"Mary Lynne is absolutely correct, class," Miss Miller interrupted, her eyes shining and pink splotches staining both of her cheeks. "Whoever wrote those words obviously wasn't listening when Mr. Stone gave the assignment."

"Perhaps," Arthur said, "but they were obviously listening closely when those other words were said to them, because they heard not only the words but the true feeling that lay behind them. That's what good dialogue is all about."

Miss Miller pressed her hands together and turned to Mr. Stone with a tight smile. "Well, time has certainly flown this morning. I'm sorry to say, Mr. Stone, that as wonderful and informative as this has been, we're going to have to wrap up now. Fifth-grade lunch period begins in a few minutes, and then I know you've got another class to visit this afternoon. Let's all thank Mr. Stone for spending time with us this morning."

Everybody clapped, and Arthur clapped for us too.

"You were great," he told us. "I hope you had a good time and maybe even picked up a couple of useful tips."

"I'm sure they did," said Miss Miller. "Those who were listening."

We were dismissed, and everyone rushed to the closets to grab lunches and jackets before heading out. As usual, I hung back, waiting for the crowd to leave, before walking over and pulling my own lunch down from the shelf.

Miss Miller was watching me, and as I stood at the closet, she leaned over to Arthur, and in a voice that sounded like a whisper but was somehow still loud enough for me to hear all the way across the room, she said, "Broken home. Absent father. You know the story."

"Yes," Arthur said nodding. "I've heard that story before."

"Haven't we all?" Miss Miller agreed.

I yanked my jacket off the hook and got out of there.

:: 13

MOST OF THE KIDS ATE LUNCH IN THE CAFETERIA AT long tables with seats attached, but I had a spot of my own, outside on a bench at the far end of the school yard, where nobody bothered me. As I headed across the yard, I thought about the exchange I had just overheard between Arthur and Miss Miller. It made me furious. What right did the two of them have to stand around talking about me as if they knew the first thing about me, all the while both of them calling me *James*? *"I've heard that story before,"* Arthur had said. What a jerk. I guess being a big-shot writer made him think he could know what somebody's story was even though he didn't know the first thing about that person. He'd probably take one look at Sapphy and think he knew her story too. He was no better than Miss Miller, and they could both rot, for all I cared.

When I reached the bench, I sat down and took out my sandwich, scraped the peanut butter out into my napkin, and ate the bread in a couple of quick, fierce bites. Then I picked up the can of cherries and turned it around, inspecting for dents. I only kept the perfect ones; the dented cans I tossed out without even bothering to open them first. I had long since stopped eating the cherries; I couldn't stand the smell of them or the feel of the soft, waterlogged globes barely contained in their slimy skin casings. I'd open the good cans, dump out the fruit, and bring the empties home. Later, after my mom had left for work and Sapphy was asleep, I'd wash them out, peel off what remained of the labels, and add them to the stash I kept behind the couch. My secret protectors.

I had begun saving cherry cans when school started up again after Christmas vacation. I figured since I slept out in the living room and didn't have a door of my own to close, I needed some kind of warning system. I set up a ring of empty cherry cans around my bed each night, and that way, if Old Gray tried to sneak up on me while I was asleep, he'd knock over the cans, and the noise would wake me up, so I'd have time to get away.

Finding no dents in the cherry can that day out in the school yard, I clamped the opener onto the lip and started to crank. I held it tightly between my knees as I worked the opener slowly all the way around the lid until it came loose and dropped down half an inch to settle on top of the cherries like a floating raft. Using my pointer finger, I placed a little pressure on one side of the lid. I had just slid my thumbnail under to pull the edge up and lift out the sharp metal circle when Audrey Krouch showed up.

"Hey," she said, "pretty quick thinking before about the squished fingers, huh?"

"You didn't have to do that," I told her.

"I know. I just figured I'd save you from getting bawled out twice in one day," she said, sitting down on the bench beside me.

I looked nervously across the playground to the basketball courts, where Larry Baywood was hanging out, shooting baskets with his friends.

"I usually eat alone," I said, hoping Audrey would take the hint and leave.

"I know," she said. Then she opened her lunch

box and pulled out a bag of chips, which she ripped open using her teeth.

"How come you didn't write a description?" she asked.

I shrugged.

"I couldn't think of anything to describe."

"Liar," she said, taking a chip from the bag and putting the whole thing in her mouth before biting down. She finished chewing and licked the salt off her fingers. "You were thinking about something. You just weren't writing it down."

"How do you know?" I asked uneasily.

"I wasn't reading your mind, if that's what you're worried about."

"Then how do you know I was thinking about something?" I asked again.

"'Cause your lips were moving," she said.

I put my hand up to my mouth. "They were?"

She nodded and ate another chip. "They always move when you think," she said. "And when you read, too."

"So?" I said defensively.

"So nothing. I'm just saying your lips move, that's all."

"You shouldn't go around trying to read people's

minds or their lips either," I said.

"It's a free country," said Audrey.

"You say that too much," I told her.

"Yeah, well, you're not exactly perfect yourself, in case you haven't noticed."

• •
• •

I missed the bus that afternoon after school. I'd gone to the library to return some books and to see if there was a copy of *Losing Perfect* I could check out. I wasn't sure why I wanted to read it. Arthur had been such a jerk, maybe I was hoping I'd find out it wasn't as good as it had seemed when he'd read it to us in class.

"I'm afraid one of your classmates was in here during lunch today and checked out the only copy we had," the librarian told me.

"Who?" I asked, even though I was sure I already knew.

"Mary Lynne Pierce," she said. "I believe she mentioned something about doing a book report for extra credit. Perhaps you could ask her to let you know when she's finished with it."

"That's okay," I said, remembering what Audrey had told me about the wart on Mary Lynne's finger. I didn't know if you could catch warts from touching pages in a book or not.

I picked out about a dozen books, some by writers I already knew I liked, others based on the descriptions on the backs of the books or the pictures on the front. I got so caught up, I lost track of the time, and when I finally finished checking out my books, the bus was gone. Wondrous Acres was a long way from school. Much too far to walk.

I tried to go back inside so I could call home. I knew my mother wouldn't appreciate being woken up, but the only other alternative was taking public transportation, and I didn't have any money with me to pay the fare. The main door of the school was locked. I knocked and knocked but nobody came. Then I remembered that Miss Miller had mentioned there was going to be a teachers' meeting after school that day, so I realized everybody must be in the auditorium. I tried the side door and the one off the gym, but all those were locked too, so I shoved as many of the books into my backpack as would fit, and splitting the rest, carrying some under each arm, I walked down the street toward the nearest city bus stop. I was hoping the driver would take pity on me and let me ride for free if I explained what had happened.

I was half a block away when I saw the blue and white bus pull into the stop up ahead and open its doors for a crowd of waiting passengers. Running as fast as I could, with the books under my arms and my backpack thumping heavily against my back, I raced toward the bus. I would have made it in time, but just as I got there, I tripped over an uneven place in the sidewalk, and my feet went out from under me. Books flew in every direction, and I came down hard on the rough cement, tearing open both knees of my jeans. It knocked the wind right out of me, and I had to lie there for a minute before I could even think about trying to stand up.

Several people bent down and started picking up the books, and someone held out a hand to help me up.

"Are you okay? That was some fall."

The soft voice was instantly familiar. I looked up to find Arthur standing over me, offering his hand. Quickly I scrambled up on my own and brushed off my pants, wincing as I touched my skinned knees. People began to hand me back my books and get on the waiting bus.

"Can I help you carry those?" Arthur asked. "Looks like you're bringing home half the library with you."

I shook my head. He smiled. Then he shrugged and pulled some change out of his pocket and stepped onto the bus. I hesitated. I wanted to get home, but I didn't want to ride with him. I didn't want to be anywhere near him.

"Are you coming, son?" the driver called out from inside. "I got a schedule to keep here."

I could have waited for the next bus, but they didn't run very often, and this driver seemed like he might be a nice guy. He'd called me "son." I tightened my grip on the books and climbed up the steps.

"I missed my school bus," I told him as soon as the door hissed closed behind me. "I don't have the fare, but if you give me the address, maybe I could send it to the bus company tomorrow."

The driver scowled and shook his head. I guess I'd read him wrong.

"First you hold up everything and now you expect a free ride?"

Arthur was sitting right behind the driver's seat, so he heard everything. He stood up and reached in his pocket.

"I've got it," he said, and came over and dropped some coins into the slot before I could object.

"I'll pay you back," I told him.

"Forget it. It's no big deal," he said, and sat back down.

• •
• •

The seats were all full except for the one beside him. I didn't know what to do. It seemed rude not to sit next to him after he'd paid my way, but I really didn't want to. The bus jerked forward, and I nearly lost my balance. With both arms full of books, there was no way to hold on.

"Why don't you put your books down here?" Arthur said, patting the empty seat next to him. There was no other choice, so I stacked the books up on the seat and then stood in the aisle, one hand on top of the pile to keep it from tipping over and the other holding on to the strap hanging from the bar above my head.

"My car's in the shop, so I got stuck taking the bus today," he said. I didn't say anything back, hoping that would be the end of it. "So you missed your bus, huh?" he went on, clearly hoping to engage me in a conversation.

"Yeah," I said, and looked around again to be sure there really weren't any other empty seats.

"It's going to take me twice as long to get home," Arthur said, "but at least I can write in my notebook. It's not safe to scribble and drive at the same time, plus this will give me a chance to look for good signs."

I wasn't sure what he was talking about, but I didn't care. All I wanted was to be left alone. Arthur reached into his pocket and pulled out his notebook and a pen. He started flipping through the pages. I looked past him, staring out the window, as we lumbered along down Main Street, stopping every two blocks or so to let people on and off.

"There's a keeper," Arthur said suddenly, pointing out the window.

We were stopped at a red light, and I looked out at the row of storefronts he was pointing at. Nothing seemed out of the ordinary to me.

"Check out the name of the beauty parlor," he told me.

I hadn't even noticed the narrow little shop wedged in between the dry cleaner's and the hardware store. There was a white sign hanging over the door that read SHEAR MAGIC, the middle of the M made out of a pair of opened scissors.

"Have you ever noticed that beauty parlors always have ridiculous names like that with bad puns in them?" Arthur said, jotting it down in his notebook. "A CUT ABOVE, MANE ATTRACTION, spelled m-a-n-e. My favorite so far, though, is CLIP JOINT. I mean, come on, who would want to call their place of business CLIP JOINT?" Arthur said with a laugh.

The bus was moving again. I could feel him looking up at me, but I pretended not to notice and stared over his head out the window.

"Look, I'm sorry about what happened this morning, James," Arthur said. "It's a common mistake, the Arthur/author thing. I've heard it a dozen times before—even from kids older than you. Please don't feel bad."

"I don't," I said.

In fact it seemed like ages ago that I'd called him Arthur in front of everybody. I didn't feel bad about it anymore, but I was still sore about the conversation with Miss Miller.

My hands were sweaty. I wiped my left palm down my pant leg. Then I let go of the strap long enough to dry my right hand too.

Arthur turned his head sideways so he could look at the titles on the spines of my library books. "Pretty eclectic taste," he said.

I didn't know what *eclectic* meant, but I didn't ask. Arthur pulled up his sleeve and looked at his watch.

"I need to get home and feed my cat." That got my attention, and I looked at him. He smiled up at me, the light catching in his glasses making them shine like two silver coins. "Do you have a cat too, James?"

"No," I said.

He tilted his head a little to one side, and my stomach lurched unexpectedly as the memory of Sapphy, the *old* Sapphy, doing that same thing flew through my mind.

"You used to have a cat, though, right?"

I had barely said two words to him. How could he possibly know about Mister?

"Do you have ESP?" I blurted out before I could stop myself.

Arthur laughed, but it wasn't a mean laugh. It was soft like the rest of his voice.

"Now that's a great question," he said. "Mostly kids ask me where my ideas come from and how many drafts I have to do before a book is finished. No, I don't have ESP. I don't even believe in it."

"Then how did you know I had a cat?" I asked.

"You told me," he said.

"No, I didn't."

"Well, not in so many words maybe, but you did tell me. You perked up a little when I mentioned my cat. Then when I asked you if you had a cat, even though you said no, the way you said it gave me a feeling that maybe you did have one once but something happened to it. The only special power I put any stock in at all is the power of observation, and all that means is looking beyond the surface of things."

I shifted uncomfortably and looked down at my feet. I was tasting butterscotch, and I knew why. I didn't like that he could see inside me like that. It felt dangerous. And familiar.

"I wasn't planning on having a cat," Arthur went on. "I'm actually more of a dog person, but when this one showed up on my doorstep out of the blue one day last fall, all bones and big eyes, I didn't have the heart to turn him away. I'm a sucker for strays."

I knew it was dumb the minute it occurred to me, but I couldn't help wondering if it was really a coincidence, the cat showing up on Arthur's doorstep like that *last fall*. Maybe it wasn't out of the blue. Maybe it was something else.

"Is your cat all black except for a little white spot right smack between his eyes?" I asked.

Arthur laughed that same soft laugh. "Good guess, but no. Jinx is an orange tabby," he said. "Marmalade-colored with bits of white."

I felt a sharp pang of disappointment, followed quickly by a flush of embarrassment. Had I actually thought it was possible that Mister wasn't really dead, that he'd walked all the way from Battle Creek to Traverse City to find me, ending up on Arthur's doorstep instead by accident?

We were getting close to my stop, so I began to gather up my books.

"You were listening today, weren't you?" Arthur said as he handed me a book off the pile.

"In class, you mean?" I said.

"No. I mean when I was talking with Miss Miller after class."

"I didn't hear anything," I lied.

"She told me your dad took off," he said.

"Yeah, so?"

"Not that it's any of my business, but for what it's worth, I know something about how that feels. My parents divorced when I was in grade school. That's where the idea for *Losing Perfect* came from."

"Is that what happened to the parents in your book, they got *divorced*?" I asked. "I thought they got snatched by aliens or something."

"No aliens. They just drop off the face of the earth. It's kind of a metaphor, you know?"

"Oh," I said. I knew what he meant. We'd talked about metaphors in class that year.

I leaned over and pulled the cord to let the driver know I wanted to get off at the next stop. Then, bracing myself with my hip against the edge of the seat to keep my balance, I gathered up the last of my books.

"Can I ask you something, James?" Arthur said.

I shrugged.

114

"Was that your dialogue I read, the one about *don't you dare?*"

"Yeah," I said uneasily.

"I thought so."

"I know I shouldn't have done it, but I couldn't think of anything else," I said.

"Shouldn't have done it? Why? You were the only one who got the point of the exercise."

"I just wrote down something somebody said to me. It's not like I thought it up myself or anything."

"I know," he said. "It was real. That's why it was so good. Ever thought about becoming a writer?"

"*Me?*" I said. "I can't write."

"I used to say that too."

"Yeah, well, I really can't write," I said. "And besides, I wouldn't want to."

I realized too late that I should have thought before I said that. He might be offended. I blushed and swallowed, but I noticed I wasn't tasting butterscotch anymore.

"I'll tell you something about writing—it changes how you feel about things," he said.

"What do you mean?"

Arthur thought for a second.

"You ever get a splinter?" he asked.

"Yeah, sure plenty of times."

"Well, you know how the second you pull it out, you feel this great sense of relief? It's kind of like that."

The bus stopped.

"This is me," I said.

Arthur smiled and lifted his hand.

"It was good talking to you, James," he said.

The doors opened, and as I started down the steps with my books tucked under my arms, I hesitated. I knew I would probably never see him again, and I also knew that I had been wrong. Arthur wasn't like Miss Miller. He wasn't like her at all.

"You getting off or what, kid?" the driver asked impatiently.

I stepped off the bus onto the road, but before the doors closed, I stuck my head in and called back to Arthur:

"My name isn't James, it's Jamie."

14 :·:

AUDREY KROUCH WAS STANDING AT THE BOTTOM OF the driveway, drinking a bottle of orange pop, when I got there. She had changed out of her stiff dress into a pair of jeans and taken her tight ponytail out, her limp hair hanging loose now, a big bump in it where the rubber band had been. She had her glasses on.

"What happened to you?" she asked, eyeing my torn jeans. "Did you miss the bus?"

"Yeah," I said. "Then I fell down running for another one."

"You're still coming over, though, right?" she said. "To get hypnotized?"

It had been a long day, and I'd forgotten all about that.

"I don't know," I said, and I started walking along the ditch toward the field.

Audrey followed me. "Aw, come on," she said. "It won't take very long. We can stop in the laundry shed, and I'll get you a bottle of pop on the way to my place."

We were in the field by then, pushing through the tall weeds.

"You should have heard Larry Baywood on the school bus this afternoon," Audrey said. "When you didn't show up, he started calling me the Black Widow and told everybody I probably ate you alive the way the spiders do. Guess what I did?"

"Beats me," I said.

"Laughed like a hyena right along with the rest of them. I acted like it was the funniest thing I'd ever heard in my life, and that shut him right up. Pretty smart, huh?"

I had to admit I would never have thought of doing that.

"I think we ought to come up with a nickname for him since he's got them for us," she said. "You got any ideas?"

I shook my head no, but a few minutes later, as we went over the top of the hill and the trailers came into view, I asked her, "Do you know what padiddle means?" She said she didn't, so I explained why

I thought it would make a good nickname for Larry.

"That's mean, making fun of somebody for having a deformed eyeball," she told me, pushing her glasses up her nose.

"I wouldn't say it to his face," I said, feeling a little ashamed.

She grinned at me.

"I would."

Audrey kept bugging me about coming over, so finally I gave in and said I would. I didn't really believe she could hypnotize people, but I figured at the very least there was an orange pop in it for me.

"I have to drop these books off at home first."

"Can I come with you?" she asked.

"No. Meet me at the shed."

She had just headed off in the opposite direction when I heard a lawn mower start up and stopped dead in my tracks. Old Gray was close by. I stood completely still until I was sure exactly which direction the sound was coming from. Then I continued walking home.

It was easiest to keep track of him when he was mowing or using the leaf blower. Otherwise

I could never be sure exactly where he was, and even though I didn't go anywhere near the office, there was always a chance I could run into him by accident coming or going from one of the trailers. It had happened several times. Once or twice he had tried to stop me, get me to talk to him, but I'd run. I'd been dumb enough to let it happen once, but I was never going to let it happen again.

I pushed open the door with my shoulder and dropped the heavy books and my backpack just inside on the floor. Sapphy must have been taking a nap in her room, because Marge was sitting at the kitchen table with her feet up on a chair, drinking one of my mother's diet colas and reading the *Star*.

"Where are you running off to in such a hurry?" she asked.

"Nowhere," I said, backing out the door and letting it slam closed behind me.

Audrey was waiting for me outside the shed when I got there.

"Somebody's inside," she said. "We better wait."

I looked in and saw a woman with pink curlers in her hair just starting to fold a huge pile of laundry. Audrey and I sat down on a bench outside the shed and started tossing pebbles at the metal trash can.

Ping!

"So what's the deal with your aunt? Is she crazy?" Audrey asked as she leaned down and scooped up a handful of gravel.

"Who told you that?"

"No one, but I've seen her. She walks around outside in her pajamas," she said, closing one eye and taking aim before letting a pebble fly.

Ping!

"Yeah, well, lots of people walk around outside wearing strange things," I said, giving her a pointed look.

"I told you already, these help me see." She pushed up her glasses.

"Well, my aunt Sapphy's not crazy. She got hit in the head and lost her memory, that's all."

"Forever?"

"Not if I can find her magic trigger," I said.

Ping!

"Nice shot. What the heck is a magic trigger?" Audrey asked, brushing the dust off her hands and turning to give me her full attention.

"It's too hard to explain." I hoped that would be enough of an answer to satisfy her, but of course it wasn't.

"Does it have anything to do with guns?"

"No."

"Magic potions?"

Audrey was a bottomless pit of questions. I decided to change the subject, grabbing up the first thing that came into my mind.

"Where does your mom get her hair cut?"

Audrey gave me a strange look.

"Why do you care?" she said.

"Does she go to Shear Magic by any chance?" I asked.

"No. I think she goes to a place called Snippity-doo-dah."

I laughed and wondered if that one was on Arthur's list.

"Does this have anything to do with magic triggers?" Audrey asked me.

"No, I was trying to change the subject."

"Why? You haven't finished telling me about the magic triggers yet."

"I don't feel like talking about that right now," I said.

"Why not?"

"Because it's private, okay? And besides, even if

I told you, you'd just keep asking me more questions about it."

"What's wrong with asking questions?"

"I don't like to answer them."

"I know," she said. "That's why you never raise your hand in class even when you know the right answer."

I sighed.

"Is there anything you *don't* think you know?"

"Yeah, I don't think I know what a magic trigger is. Not yet anyway."

The woman in the curlers finally finished her folding and emerged with a basket piled high with clean laundry. We waited until she was out of sight; then we went inside, and Audrey walked over and kicked the machine.

"How'd you learn how to do that, anyway?" I asked, taking a swig from the ice-cold bottle of pop she had handed me.

"I figured it out by accident. I was in a bad mood one day and felt like kicking something. I got lucky and hit the right spot. Don't tell anybody though, okay?"

"I won't," I said.

"Can you imagine what would happen if the manager found out? What's his-name in the office, you know, the guy with the gray hair."

"Call me Old Gray," he said the day I helped him hang up his Christmas lights. "That's what all my friends call me."

"I know who you mean," I said, doing my best to keep my voice even. "I think his name is Mr. Greene."

"Yeah. Anyway, what if Mr. Greene found out and called the cops on me? My mom would hit the roof. You want another one before we go?" Audrey asked, nodding toward the pop machine.

"No, thanks." I held up my half-empty bottle. "I haven't finished this one yet."

We turned right out of the shed and started walking toward Audrey's place. I didn't even have time to think about how weird it had felt when she brought up Old Gray, because right away she was firing more questions at me. One thing I will say about Audrey Krouch's questions, they weren't like anybody else's.

"How much would you charge to eat a pine-cone?"

"What kind of thing is that to ask a person?" I said.

"What's wrong with it? All I want to know is how much you'd charge," she said.

"Why would I charge anything?"

"You mean you'd eat a pinecone for *free*?" she asked.

"No, I mean I wouldn't eat a pinecone at all."

"I would, for a million bucks. Wouldn't you?"

"For a million bucks? Sure," I said.

"How 'bout for a thousand?"

I tipped my bottle up and drained the last couple of inches of sweet pop.

"Yeah, I'd do it for a thousand," I said, wiping my mouth on my sleeve. "But who's going to pay me a thousand bucks to eat a pinecone?"

"There are a lot of kooks in the world."

"I can think of one I know right now," I said, shooting her a sideways look.

"Very funny. This is it." She pointed to a white trailer on our left, the last one in the row. "The car's not there, which means my mom isn't home."

"Maybe she's out getting you pinecones for dinner," I said.

Audrey laughed and ran on ahead and up the steps of the rickety little porch of unit number fifteen. When I caught up with her, she was fumbling with her house key, which was tied to the zipper of her backpack with a long gray shoelace. She put the key in the lock and jiggled it a few times until finally it turned.

It's funny how every house has its own special smell. Funnier still how hard it is to describe that smell, even when it's your own house. I could draw you a picture of our place in Battle Creek, where every window and door was and how the furniture was set up, but when I try to think of how to describe what it smelled like when I walked in the door, the only word I can come up with is *home*. Audrey's house smelled oniony, like her.

The layout of the trailer was identical to Sapphy's, but it felt completely different. For one thing, it was dark. There were heavy curtains on all the windows, and the furniture was big and hulking. It was like a cave crowded with boulders.

"You want something to eat before we start?" Audrey asked. "My mom made a cake last night.

Chocolate with marshmallow frosting. There's probably some left, unless she ate it for lunch."

I'd seen Audrey's mom around. Lucille Krouch was a large woman with short, frizzy hair dyed bright orange. She had a gap between her front teeth and a loud laugh, and she drove a big old boat of a Chevy, which rode so low to the ground, it sometimes scraped bottom.

I shook my head. Now that I was actually standing alone with Audrey in her oniony living room, I was feeling pretty nervous.

"Maybe I should go," I said, taking a step toward the door.

"Why? You want to get hypnotized, don't you?"

"I don't know," I said.

"Come on. It won't take very long."

"How long?" I asked.

"That depends on how susceptible you are," said Audrey.

"How *susceptible?*"

"Yeah, how easy you are to put under. I can find that out by asking you some questions."

"What kind of questions?" I asked warily.

"Don't worry, they're easy ones," she said. "Wait a second, I'll get the book."

Audrey walked over to a set of shelves jammed with paperbacks, pulled out a tall yellow book, and quickly flipped to a page near the front.

"Here we go," she said. "Question number one: Do you take in strays?"

"Wait a minute. I thought you said you knew how to do this," I said.

"I do."

"Then why do you need that book?"

"It's just like using a cookbook. That doesn't mean you don't know how to cook. It just means you haven't memorized the recipes. So answer the question. Have you ever taken in a stray animal?"

It was funny, Audrey's asking me that after Arthur had just told me he was a sucker for strays.

"Yes," I said. "A cat."

"I love cats. My mom won't let me have one, though, because she's allergic. What's your cat's name?" she asked.

I hesitated. There wasn't a day that passed that I didn't think about Mister, but I hadn't realized until that moment how long it had been since I'd actually said his name out loud. A hard lump rose in my throat, and I had to swallow it back down before I could answer.

"Mister," I said. "But he's dead."

"Oh," said Audrey, "that's too bad. Well, taking in strays is one of the signs that you're susceptible to hypnosis, so that's good anyway. How about question number two: Do you ever cry at movies?"

I often cried at sad books, and I'd come close to crying a couple of times listening to Frank Sinatra sing "Mood Indigo," but luckily she had only asked me about movies.

"No," I answered truthfully.

"Okay, there are just a few more questions."

What was I doing here? Audrey Krouch wasn't a real hypnotist. She didn't know any magic words, and she wasn't going to be able to help me. She was just a kid, and I didn't want to answer any more of her dumb questions.

"I'm going to get going," I said again.

"Wait," said Audrey. "I kept my part of the bargain; I got you the pop. We can skip the rest of the questions. Stay here and I'll get my stuff."

I could have left. It's not as if she could have stopped me—not physically anyway. Instead I stayed, and while I waited for her to come back, I went over and looked at the collection of framed photographs arranged in a semicircle on the table behind the couch. There were pictures of Audrey at various stages of childhood and Lucille Krouch, always smiling directly into the camera, looking exactly the same in every shot except for the color of her hair, which seemed to have been every color imaginable at some point along the way. I noticed there were no pictures of the dad Audrey had written her description about, but I figured that was probably because he'd been the one behind the camera, taking all those pictures of his great big wife and their goofy-looking kid.

"Back," Audrey said, coming into the room a minute later with a shoe box in her hands. She set the box on the coffee table and went into the kitchen, where she opened a drawer and rummaged around for a minute before pulling out a large slotted spoon. She breathed on it, then polished it with the edge of her T-shirt.

"What's that for?" I asked.

She came over to me and started slowly swinging the spoon by the handle back and forth in front of my face.

I snorted. "You've gotta be kidding. Don't you know you're supposed to use a watch on a chain when you hypnotize somebody?"

"Shows what you know," she said. "It doesn't matter what I use, just so long as you keep your eyes on it. You can look it up in the book if you don't believe me."

"I don't care what your book says, I don't want to look at that dirty spoon. Doesn't your dad have an old watch lying around here someplace?"

A strange look passed over Audrey's face.

"Look, do you want me to hypnotize you or not?"

I was a little surprised by the sudden change in her tone. She sounded mad.

"Take off your shoes and lie down on the couch," she said.

"You want me to lie down?" I said uneasily.

I had the same feeling about lying on the Krouches' musty old couch as I did about sitting on the rug at school, and I wasn't too crazy about the

131

idea of taking my shoes off either. The floor was covered in a shaggy carpet that looked as if it hadn't been vacuumed in a while.

"Is it okay if I just stand up instead?" I asked.

"No. You have to lie down so you can relax and empty your mind, or I won't be able to enter it."

Audrey Krouch was skinny as a stick and at least two inches taller than I was. A sudden image of her trying to gather up her gangly legs and arms and "enter" my mind, like a giraffe crawling into a car window, made it hard to keep from laughing.

"How about if I just sit here like this?" I asked, taking a seat on the edge of the couch and folding my hands in my lap.

"Fine," said Audrey, rolling her eyes. "Are you ready now?"

She opened the shoe box and took out a candle and a small blue glass bottle. She lit the candle, but it was so little, it didn't make the room any brighter. Still, there's something about candles burning that makes it feel as if something important is happening, and for the first time since I'd walked in the door, I had to be honest with myself. Even though I knew Madame Yerdua was only plain old Audrey Krouch, there was still a part of me that believed she might be able to help me forget.

:: 15

AUDREY PICKED UP THE LITTLE BLUE BOTTLE AND unscrewed the cap. Holding her index finger over the top, she tipped it twice quickly and wet her fingertip before touching me lightly in the middle of my forehead and at the corner of each eye. The smell was familiar, but it took me a second to place it. Sapphy kept several bottles of perfume and lotions on her dresser top. I had opened them all one night, dabbing her wrists and spritzing the air in search of magic triggers. This same perfume had been there among them. I was sure of it. I remembered because the smell had been so much sweeter and stronger than the rest, almost overwhelming. I had looked at the label to see what it was called. Attar of roses.

Audrey put the cap back on the bottle and picked up the spoon.

"Before we can begin, you have to tell me why you want to be hypnotized," she said, and she didn't sound mad anymore.

"No more questions," I told her. "Come on. Let's just do it."

"I have to ask this one. Otherwise how am I supposed to know what posthypnotic suggestion to plant?" she explained.

"What's a posthypnotic suggestion?"

"It's, like, say you're a nail biter, right? And you want to stop biting your nails? I put you under, and then I tell you not to bite your nails anymore," Audrey said.

"And that's it?" I said.

"Pretty much."

Could it really be that simple? Was it a post-hypnotic suggestion that had made my grandfather bark like a dog at the county fair and then forget that he had ever done it? The small ember of hope, which had first sparked to life as I'd stood in the laundry shed looking at the blue flyer, began to glow more brightly now.

"You just tell me what to do and I do it?" I asked.

"Yep," said Audrey. "So what do you want?"

It was such a simple question, I answered it without hesitating. Like opening a door without bothering to ask first, "Who's there?"

"I want to forget," I said.

"Forget what?" she asked.

Obviously I should have anticipated this question, especially from Audrey. But I had gotten caught up in the candlelight and the hopefulness and let my guard down by accident. Quickly I scrambled for cover.

"I didn't mean that. What I meant was, I don't want to forget, I want to learn why people forget, so I can help my aunt get her memory back."

Audrey was watching me closely. "I thought you said you were going to do that with those trigger things," she said.

"We are. But maybe there's something else we can do while we're looking for the triggers."

"So let me get this straight. You *don't* want to forget something?" she said.

"No," I said, shaking my head adamantly. "What would I need to do that for? I'm not the one with the memory problem. It's my aunt. I'm doing this for her. Not me."

"Huh," she said. "Well, that's kind of confusing

then, 'cause why am I hypnotizing you? Sounds like I should be hypnotizing her."

"Sapphy? No. That would never work," I said. "And besides, it could be dangerous. You might do something wrong and make her even worse. Why don't you just hypnotize me, say something about forgetting, and let me worry about what happens after that."

"It doesn't really work like that," she said as she reached for the yellow book, which lay facedown on the table, still opened up to the page of questions.

"Can't we at least try it?" I asked. "Please?"

She hesitated for a minute, then left the book where it was.

"I guess," she said. "If that's really what you want to do."

"Thanks," I said, my heart pounding as if I'd just stepped off the curb and narrowly missed being hit by a car. I was hopeful that she could help me, but that didn't mean I was willing to tell her why I needed her help.

Audrey picked up the big metal spoon and began to swing it slowly back and forth in front of my face. She told me not to take my eyes off it no matter what, and so I watched it swing back and forth, back and forth.

"Your eyelids are feeling heavy now. You wish that you could close them. You wish that you could sleep. But it's not time yet. It's not time. Soon it will be time to sleep. Soon it will be time. But not yet."

At first it was hard not to laugh. Audrey Krouch was swinging a big spoon in my face and telling me not to go to sleep. It was ridiculous. But I bit my lip and didn't laugh because I knew it would make her mad, and if she got mad, she might change her mind about trying it my way.

And then I didn't feel like laughing anymore. At first I thought maybe it was my imagination, but then I realized, no, it was true, my eyelids *were* beginning to feel a little heavy. As if two cool copper pennies were resting on top of them, pushing them closed as I fought to keep them open.

"Not yet," said Audrey quietly, "not yet. But very soon."

Pennies, or maybe fingertips. But whose fingers were they? Audrey's? My own? I struggled to keep my eyes open. Back and forth. Back and forth went the spoon. Sapphy would have liked the way the light caught in the metal and sparkled as it swung. Back and forth. Back and forth. If only I could close my eyes. Just for a minute. If only I could sleep.

"You may close your eyes now," Audrey said softly, and she put down the spoon and reached for the yellow book on the table. I was so relieved to finally be able to shut my eyes, I forgot all about my feelings about the musty couch and lay right down, sinking deep into the soft cushions. I didn't even mind it when I felt Audrey untie my shoes and pull them off. "I want you to imagine that you are on a sandy beach. Warm sun shines down on you, caressing your body with its healing light. Gentle waves lap at the shore, and a moist, cool sea breeze blows through your hair." I had a feeling Audrey must be reading from the yellow book, because the words didn't sound like things she would actually say. She went on in a soft, dreamy voice. "In the distance you see a tall building. That is your destination. The tall building. Your feet walk effortlessly upon the warm sand. Almost as though you are gliding."

I was still listening to Audrey's voice, but I was also picturing myself on the beach, gliding along toward the tall building. I was moving so smoothly, my feet barely touched the ground. The sun poured over me like warm syrup and the waves sparkled and Audrey's voice seemed to come from somewhere far away, out where the blue of the sea met the blue of the sky and they both just kept going.

"You are focused on the building. That is your destination. You are almost there. I want you to stop walking and take three deep breaths with me now."

I lay on the couch, with my eyes closed tight, and took three slow, deep breaths, exhaling through my mouth each time.

"You are walking again. You are walking upon the warm sand. And now, at last, you reach the tall building," Audrey continued in her faraway voice. "As you enter, you notice a large elevator on your right. You can see yourself reflected in the shiny metal doors. Do you see yourself in the doors?"

I did see myself. Like in a dream.

"Mmm-hmm," I murmured softly.

"Good. Now the doors slide open, and you enter the elevator. The number ten lights up as the elevator doors close. The car begins to move. You are going down. You see the numbers light up in red as you descend. Down, down, down you go, and the numbers go down too. Ten . . . nine . . . eight . . ."

She counted slowly all the way down to one.

"And now you have arrived. You are all the way down. All the way down under the ground, where it is safe and warm. You can relax now and be at peace with yourself."

I was floating a million miles away. I could hear her voice, so I knew I was still awake, but it was as if I were sound asleep at the same time. It felt so good, I didn't want it ever to end. I wanted to keep floating like that forever and never have to come back. Everything would get smaller and smaller, just the way the house in Battle Creek had after we drove away from it for the last time. I wanted to keep floating until no matter where I looked, there was nothing to see but clear blue water, and then I would close my eyes, take a deep breath, and finally let myself forget. . . .

. . . *the way Old Gray always seemed to be sitting out on the office steps when I came home from school each day. How he'd wave to me and start up a conversation as I walked past. And then how one day he said if I would help him hang up his Christmas lights, he'd give me five dollars. I said sure, and I put down my books and climbed up on the ladder to help him hang the strings of colored bulbs from the rain gutters.*

While we worked, Old Gray asked me all kinds of questions. What was my favorite subject at school? Did I have a best friend? And how did I feel about not having a father around anymore? I told him that my mom didn't like it when I talked about my dad, but Old Gray said he didn't mind a bit if I wanted to talk about my dad. In fact I could talk about him all day long if I wanted to, and he promised he would never tell my mother. "Trust me," he said. "It will be our secret."

He was so easy to talk to. He made me feel like I was the most important person in the world. He kept asking me questions, and I kept telling him things. How I hadn't made any friends at school yet. How Mister had died and how I missed my dad and couldn't understand why he hadn't at least called me to see how I was doing. "My mother says he's good for nothing," I told him, "but he's still my dad, and Christmas isn't going to feel right without him." I told him that my mother said she didn't feel like celebrating, so we weren't even going to have a tree, and Old Gray said that gave him an idea. How would it be, he asked me, if he got a Christmas tree for the office and I came over and helped him decorate it on Christmas Eve, just the two of us? I said I thought that sounded like a great idea. I liked Old Gray, and I could tell he liked me too. He cared about what mattered to me, and somehow he seemed to understand how I felt even without my telling him. We finished hanging up his lights, and I helped him fold up the ladder and carry it around back to the toolshed. Before I left, he put his arm around my shoulders and told me that if he had a son like me, wild horses couldn't drag him away. "By the way," he said as he pulled a crisp five-dollar bill out of his wallet and handed it to me, "what's your favorite candy, Jamie?"

"Butterscotch," I told him.

After that, Old Gray talked about the Christmas tree every time I saw him. At first he said he was going to get a really big one, like the ones I'd told him we'd always had in Battle Creek. But then he decided it might be more special to get a live tree instead of a dead one off the lot. He told me the *live trees weren't as big as the chopped-down kind, but that it wouldn't matter—we would still be able to decorate it with candy canes and tinsel when I came over on Christmas Eve.*

"And I've got a present for you too, Jamie," Old Gray told me, "something I know you're going to like."

Old Gray asked me not to tell anyone about our tree-trimming party. He said he didn't want the other kids at Wondrous Acres to find out and feel bad that they hadn't been invited. So after dinner on Christmas Eve, while my mom was busy giving Sapphy a bath and getting her ready for bed, I told her I was going for a walk, slipped out of the house, and headed over to Old Gray's office. I figured it wouldn't take long to decorate the tree—Old Gray said it would be small. I was sure I'd be back home by the time my mom was finished with Sapphy.

There was about a foot of snow on the ground, and I stamped my boots on the steps while I waited for him to answer the door. It suddenly occurred to me that if Old Gray had a present for me, maybe I was supposed to have one for him too. I felt bad, but it was too late to do anything about it. He opened the door and told me to come inside. I followed him into the back room where the tree was. It was sitting on a table in a shiny red plastic pot. Even though he had warned me that it would be small, I was surprised by how little it really was. More like a houseplant than a Christmas tree. Still, we managed to wind a string of miniature lights around it and hang tiny candy canes and tinsel on the thin branches.

It had always been my job at home to put the star on the top of the tree. When I was little, my father would scoop me up in his arms and hoist me over his head so that I could reach. Later I would stand on the kitchen step stool while my mother held it steady, one hand on the stool, the other on the small of my back, all the while warning me to be careful not to fall.

"We need something for the top," I told Old Gray.

Old Gray said he'd forgotten about that part, but we managed to dig up a tinfoil ashtray, and I cut it into a star shape and pinned it to the top of the tree with a paper clip. Then we turned off the lights and plugged in the tree so we could admire our handiwork.

"Pretty Christmassy, huh?" he said, beaming at me in the dim glow of the little lights.

"Pretty Christmassy." I agreed.

"Ready for your present?" he asked, and from behind his back he brought out a big bag of butterscotch candies with a red ribbon tied around it. "Have one," he said. "They're your favorites. See how I remembered that? I know what you like, don't I?"

I thanked him and took the bag from him and poked a hole in it with my finger. I pulled out one of the cellophane-wrapped candies, untwisted the ends, and popped it into my mouth. I sucked on it for a second, then pushed the smooth buttery candy into my cheek with my tongue so I could speak.

"Want one?" I asked, holding out the bag to him.

Old Gray shook his head and smiled. "Those are for you." Then he put his arm around my shoulders, just the way he'd done that day I'd helped him hang up his lights.

Only this time he left his arm there a little too long, and when I started to feel uncomfortable and tried to move away, he tightened his grip.

"What are you doing?" I said.

"I want to be your friend, Jamie."

But it wasn't true. He didn't want to be my friend. He didn't want to be my friend at all. When I tried again to get away, he got his arm around my neck and pulled me in tight against him, one of the buttons on his shirt pressing hard into my cheek. His hair was gray, but he wasn't an old man—he was strong. "I love you, Jamie," he said. I must have swallowed the candy whole at some point as I struggled to get free, or maybe I spit it out. I don't remember. All I remember is that I could still taste it. And I'd been tasting butterscotch ever since.

"Did you say butterscotch?" Audrey asked softly.

Suddenly I couldn't breathe. I wasn't floating anymore; I was drowning. I opened my eyes, and I wasn't in the ocean or riding in the silver elevator. I was lying on Audrey Krouch's dirty old couch with my shoes off, and I had just told her what I had sworn I would never tell anyone. I jumped up, knocking over the candle in my panic.

"Hey, watch it!" Audrey cried, grabbing for the candle, as hot wax spilled out onto the tabletop. "What's the matter with you?"

"How could you do that?" I shouted.

"What are you talking about?"

"You tricked me. You tricked me into telling you."

"I didn't trick you into anything. You asked me to hypnotize you, so I did. I can't help it if it worked."

I picked up my shoes and jammed my feet into them, but my fingers were shaking so badly, I couldn't tie the laces.

"If you tell anyone what I told you, I'll break your neck, Audrey Krouch. I mean it, I really will."

"But you didn't tell me anything," she said.

"You're lying," I said.

"No, I'm not. Your lips were moving the whole time, but the only thing you said out loud was 'butterscotch.' Why would I tell anybody that? It doesn't even mean anything."

"Swear it," I said, balling my hands into fists and taking a menacing step toward her. "Swear that it's all I said."

"I swear," said Audrey, quickly drawing an X over her heart with her finger. "Butterscotch. That's it."

I had never hit anybody in my life, but I wanted to hit Audrey Krouch. I hated her for knowing all the things she knew about me that I had never intended to tell her. But besides being mad, I was also confused. Mixed in with the relief I felt when Audrey swore I hadn't told her anything was a devastating sense of disappointment. Nothing had changed. The burden of the terrible secret I had just so vividly relived was still mine alone to bear.

I'm glad I didn't hit her—it would have been the wrong thing to do—but I'm not proud of what I did next. I snatched the glasses right off her face, and clutching them tightly in my fist, I turned and ran home.

:: 16

THAT NIGHT I SKIPPED DINNER. I TOLD MY MOTHER I felt sick, and it was true. She opened up the couch and made up my bed for me early and brought me a cool washcloth to put on my forehead. I lay there by myself while she and Sapphy ate dinner together out in the kitchen. Later, after she had cleared the table, my mother turned on the radio so she could listen while she did the dishes. The dial was set to the Motown station I had been listening to that morning, but she began to turn it, looking for one of her golden oldies stations instead. All of a sudden, out of the static Frank Sinatra's voice came floating out into the room.

"Boy, does this take me back," said Sapphy. "Nobody sings like Old Blue Eyes."

If the song had been "Mood Indigo," I probably wouldn't have been able to hold it together. I was that close to the edge. I would have cried, my mother would have come over and asked me what the matter was, and then who knows what would have happened? Luckily, though, Frank was singing "Fly Me to the Moon."

Before she left for work, my mother came and sat on the edge of my bed.

"I need to get going," she said. "I gave Sapphy her pill early, and she's already tucked in. Get some rest, cowboy. You probably caught that bug that's going around. If you don't feel better in the morning, you can stay home from school, okay?"

Then she leaned over and kissed me right above the ear. I didn't move. I lay there, holding my breath, afraid if I breathed in even the tiniest bit of her, a whiff of her hand lotion or the cigarette smoke that clung to her hair, I would break into a million pieces, like a jigsaw puzzle being lifted up by the edges.

After my mother left, I threw off the covers and got out of bed. Then I went and got Audrey's glasses out of my backpack where I'd stashed them and walked quickly down the hallway to the bathroom.

I don't know what I expected to see as I stood in front of the mirror and slipped those glasses on. Something that would explain how she knew about the cherry cans and the reason I didn't walk on the driveway, I guess. But all I saw was my own pale, miserable self staring back at me, Audrey's big black glasses sliding down my nose. I stood for a while, looking into the mirror. Then I took the glasses off and, holding them in both hands, snapped them in two.

Back in the living room I shoved the broken glasses under my pillow, took the cherry cans out from behind the couch, and began to set them up around my bed. When I had finished, I crawled under the covers and lay in the dark, listening for footsteps. Outside, the wind set the trees swaying, and the moon sent shadowy fingers from their branches dancing through the window and across the walls. After a while I finally managed to doze off.

In the middle of the night Sapphy woke up. She

got out of bed and, groggy from her medication, got turned around, somehow ending up out in the living room. She stumbled in the dark, and I woke up, heart pounding wildly, to the terrible clattering I had feared for months would come.

"Get away from me!" I screamed. "Don't touch me! Get away!"

"Who is that?" Sapphy whispered in the dark. "Who's there?"

As soon as I realized what had happened, I got quickly out of bed.

"It's me, Sapphy. It's Jamie. I'm sorry if I scared you. Go back to bed," I told her.

But Sapphy didn't go back to bed. Instead, she fumbled around and managed to switch on the light. We both stood there blinking, in the glare, at the empty cherry cans scattered across the floor in every direction, some lying on their sides like fallen soldiers, others still bravely standing guard.

"What is all this?" she asked.

"It's nothing," I said, bending down and righting one of the cans. "It's just something I have to do, that's all."

"Why, Jamie?" Sapphy asked, and as she looked at me, she slowly tilted her poor bedraggled-looking head to one side, like a crow. "What's happened?"

Later I would wonder why I hadn't realized right away what it meant when Sapphy tilted her head like that. I guess I was too busy trying to hold myself together to notice. When I got down on my hands and knees and began to set the cans back up, Sapphy came over and got down beside me to help. When we had finished, she went and turned out the light. Then, careful not to knock over the cans, she lifted the edge of her robe, stepped over the barrier, and came to sit beside me on the bed.

"You can tell me," she said.

It felt like one of those times when you spend hours turning everything upside down looking for your hat, only to realize it's been sitting on your head the whole time. Sapphy was right—I could tell her. She was the one person in the world who wouldn't hold it against me, because the next day she wouldn't even be able to remember it.

"Tell me everything," she said.

And so I did.

• •
• •

When I had finished, Sapphy was quiet.

"I'm sorry," I whispered.

"You've got nothing to be sorry for," said Sapphy.

"I shouldn't have gone there," I said. "It was dumb."

"It's not your fault what happened. It's not your fault, Jamie."

I cried then. The hard kind of crying. The kind that hurts on the way out and comes in waves from deep inside. It made my head pound and ripped my throat raw, but I didn't try to stop it. I needed to cry, almost as much as I'd needed to tell someone the awful thing that had happened to me. In the morning Sapphy wouldn't remember what I'd told her, and she wouldn't remember what she'd said to me either, but I would never forget it. *It was not my fault.*

"Come here," Sapphy said, her eyes glittering with tears as she opened her arms wide for me. The loose sleeves of her robe hung down, and in the dark they looked like giant wings. I laid my head against her chest, and when she folded her arms around me and began to rock, I closed my eyes and imagined that she was the bird from my dream, lifting me up and carrying me off to safety.

17 ::

IT WASN'T OLD BLUE EYES WHO FINALLY GOT Sapphy's memory to jump the scratch. It was me. Who would have guessed that what we hadn't been able to find in the spice rack or the photo albums or the back of the closet would lie in the painful butterscotch-flavored secret I told her that night. If Audrey hadn't made me wish I had talked, or if Frank Sinatra had sung a different song that night on the radio, things might have been different. But Sapphy heard me calling to her over the clatter of empty cherry cans, and she tilted her head to the side and followed the sound of my voice all the way home.

It was four o'clock in the morning when my mother came in and found Sapphy sitting on my bed, stroking my hair as I lay sleeping peacefully in her lap, a ring of empty cans on the floor around us. I had told Sapphy everything, and Sapphy had done the one thing I had counted on her not to do: She had remembered. I never had to see the look on my mother's face when she heard what had happened to me, because it was Sapphy who told her, not me.

A whole lot happened pretty quickly after that. For one thing, the police came, and after asking me a lot of very hard questions, they took Old Gray away. My mom decided to take some time off from her job, to stay home with Sapphy and me. She even cooked a pot roast one night. We could have used Grandma Jeanne's gravy boat, but we made do with a bowl and a spoon, and I don't think anybody minded at all. Sapphy was sad to learn that she had broken all her dishes, but she talked my mother into unpacking our share of the bone china, and after that we used it every day.

I missed a week of school, and by then it was Easter vacation, so I didn't have to go back for another two weeks anyway. Mostly I stayed inside except for when we went into town to meet with Mr. Uhl, the lawyer my mother had hired to help us when my case went to trial.

Apparently it wasn't the first time Old Gray had done something like this, but I like to think it was the last.

Sapphy's memory was back for good, so Marge didn't have to come anymore, though it would still be a while before she was completely herself again. My mom and I took some long walks together, and we had some long talks, too. We even talked about my dad. She told me he had called a couple of times and asked if it would be okay to come visit us. She said she was sorry she hadn't told me about the calls; she hadn't wanted to get my hopes up or hers either. The next time he called, she promised, she'd tell him it was okay to come.

One afternoon, the phone rang. It was the pound, calling to let Sapphy know they finally had a beagle puppy for her. Sapphy and that dog hit it off the minute they laid eyes on each other. After trying out a couple of names for him, she settled on Bert, short for Sherbert. While Sapphy talked to the people at the pound, I heard the mailman toot his horn down on the road, and for the first time in a long time I actually walked down the driveway. I ran into Audrey Krouch on my way back up.

"Hey," she said.

"Hey, yourself," I said, and kept walking. I hadn't seen her since the afternoon she'd hypnotized me, and I felt embarrassed about the way I'd acted in front of her.

"I heard about what happened. About them taking that creep away. It's all anybody can talk about around here anymore," Audrey said as she turned around and started following me back up the driveway.

"Are you mad at me?" she asked.

"I don't know. I don't think so," I said.

"Either you're mad or you're not. Which is it?"

"Not, I guess."

"Good," she said. "Now don't you want to know if I'm mad at you?"

"Are you?" I said.

"That depends on whether you plan to give me back my glasses."

I felt a guilty twist in my stomach. There was no way around it. I had to tell her.

"I broke them."

"Why'd you do that?" she said.

"I'm sorry. I couldn't help it. I was mad."

I expected her to be angry, to insult me or yell

at me or maybe even try to push me down, but I didn't expect her to cry. I stood there uncomfortably watching her. I didn't have a Kleenex to offer her, and I couldn't think of anything to say to make it better. Finally she stopped and wiped her nose on her sleeve.

"They belonged to my father," she said.

"Tell him I'll pay him back," I told her.

"I can't. I don't even know him. He left before I was born."

"What about all that stuff you wrote about driving around in the car with him?" I asked. "Playing the radio and looking at the maps?"

"I made it all up."

I was shocked. "I totally believed you," I said.

"I'm sorry."

"No, that's okay," I told her. "It was just all so believable, I'm surprised, that's all. You could have told me the truth, you know."

"I just did," she said.

We started walking up the driveway again.

"Can I ask you something, Audrey?" I said after a while.

"Sure."

"How did you know about the cherry cans?"

"All I know about cherry cans is that every day at lunch you either throw the whole can away or you open it, throw the cherries out, and keep the can," Audrey told me. "And while we're at it, I might as well tell you that I also know you don't really read on the bus, you don't like peanut butter, and for some reason you save gum wrappers."

"You don't have ESP," I said. "You've been spying on me."

"Not spying. Looking. It's a free country. I can look at whoever I want."

"But why do you want to look at me?" I said.

She blushed a deep pink.

"You figure it out," she told me.

I had a feeling I just had, and I blushed too.

"By the way," Audrey said, "I may not have ESP, but I sure hypnotized the heck out of you."

"You did not," I said. "I was awake the whole time."

"Oh, yeah? Then why were you drooling?" asked Audrey.

"I wasn't."

"Oh, yes, you were, right down your chin. You came over to my house and lay down on the couch, and I hypnotized you until you drooled like a baby, and if you don't want me telling everybody that, then you'd better just admit it right now."

"Fine," I said. "You hypnotized me."

She grinned. "I did, didn't I?"

We had reached the top of the driveway, and Old Gray's office stood in front of us. The yellow police tape had been removed, but there was a heavy iron padlock on the front door.

"I have an idea," Audrey said. "Let's grab some rocks off that pile over there and break all the windows. Even if we get caught, nobody will blame us. Not after what he did."

I will always have a soft spot in my heart for Audrey Krouch for having suggested that. And who knows, maybe it would have done me some good to hurl a few rocks through Old Gray's windows. But when I looked over at the pile of stones Audrey was pointing to, something else caught my eye. A quick flash of red among the weeds. Audrey saw it too.

"What is that?" she said.

I knew what it was.

"It's nothing," I told her. "Come on, let's go."

I put my hand on her shoulder, but Audrey shook it loose, ran over, and bent down in the weeds.

"Come look at this! It's a Christmas tree!" she called out to me.

"No, it's not," I called back.

"Yes, it is. It's got Christmas lights on it. Come see for yourself if you don't believe me."

The bottom branches were dried up and had lost all their needles, and the dirt around the trunk was hard as cement, but the little tree was still alive. In fact there was even some new pale-green growth on the very top where I had once pinned the tin ashtray star. The star and the candy canes were long gone, but a few strands of tinsel clung to the branches, and the string of lights was still wrapped around it, a couple of feet of green cord with a plug on the end dangling out of the pot like a forked tail.

"I've got an idea. Let's plant it," Audrey said.

I didn't move.

"Come on. Let's plant it, so it won't die."

"I don't care if it dies," I said.

Audrey looked over at me.

"Oh," she said, and stood up, taking a quick step backward. I guess she finally realized who it had belonged to.

We stood there for a minute, looking at it. Then I walked over to the tree, and after snatching off the few remaining bits of tinsel, I took hold of the dangling cord and yanked off the lights, which I flung as far as I could into the weeds. There was nothing Christmassy about it anymore. Now it was just a tree—a tree that needed to be planted or it would die. For some reason I thought about Arthur then. About his notebook full of observations and his round glasses and what he'd said about the splinter. I crouched down and took hold of the edges of the red pot.

"Pull it out," I said.

Audrey grabbed the tree by the middle of its thin trunk and easily tugged it free of the pot.

"Now what?" she said.

We carried the tree back to Sapphy's trailer, where Audrey helped me dig a hole. Together we planted it in a sunny spot beside the porch.

"It looks pretty scrawny now, but maybe by

Christmas it'll look good enough to decorate," Audrey said as she patted down the earth around the trunk.

I shook my head. "We're going to have a real Christmas tree next year," I told her. "Not this one. A big fat one, just like always."

I went inside to get a pan of water to pour around the tree. There was a note on the table from my mother saying that she and Sapphy had gone to pick up the new puppy. When I came back outside, I had Audrey's broken glasses in my hand.

"Maybe we could tape them back together," I said as I handed them to her.

"Maybe," she said. But instead she squatted down, and using her fingers, she dug a small hole in the freshly turned earth beneath the little tree and pushed the glasses down into it.

"Come on," said Audrey as she stood up and brushed the dirt off her hands. "I'll teach you how to kick that pop machine if you want."

"Okay," I said.

As we set off for the laundry shed together that afternoon, I tipped my head back and looked up at the sky. It was clear and bright and a normal-as-cornflakes shade of blue I hadn't seen in a very long time.

"I should warn you," Audrey told me. "No matter how you do it, that machine only gives orange."

"I like orange."

"I know," she said. "Me too."

Sarah Weeks is an award-winning author of many books for children. Her most recent novel, *So B. It*, was named an ALA Notable Children's Book and a Top 10 Best Book for Young Adults. She has also written the popular Guy series, including *Regular Guy*, *Guy Wire*, *Guy Time*, and *My Guy*, which is soon to be a feature film by Disney. Sarah Weeks grew up in Michigan and now lives in New York City with her two teenaged sons. You can visit her online at www.sarahweeks.com.